THE
ALIENS
WILL COME TO
GEORGIA FIRST

STORIES

THE ALIENS
WILL COME TO
GEORGIA FIRST
STORIES

STEPHEN HUNDLEY

UNG
UNIVERSITY of
NORTH GEORGIA™
UNIVERSITY PRESS

Blue Ridge | Cumming | Dahlonega | Gainesville | Oconee

Published by:
University of North Georgia Press
Dahlonega, Georgia

Printing Support by:
Lightning Source Inc.
La Vergne, Tennessee

Cover design by Sam Caldwell.
Book design by Corey Parson.

ISBN: 978-1-940771-78-6

Printed in the United States of America
For more information, please visit: http://ung.edu/university-press
Or e-mail: ungpress@ung.edu

Dedicated to my mother and first editor, Dr. Sheri Hundley.

Lord, we have come to the end
Of this kind of vision of heaven
    —James Dickey, "For the Last Wolverine"

CONTENTS

Acknowledgments

The author is indebted to the following literary magazines for their generosity and faith in these stories.

"Dog" and "The War of Naked Aggression" were initially published in *BULL: Men's Fiction*, "Elsohn" in *The MacGuffin*, "Snowbirds" in *Waxwing*, "Black Bird" in *Permafrost*, and "The Aliens Will Come to Georgia First" in *Carve Magazine*.

"Settled" was awarded the 2019 Larry Brown Short Story Award by *Pithead Chapel*.

SETTLED

After it's finished and I am cradling the back of her head, filled with the rhythm of her long and easy breathing, the gentle spasms that make her shoulders twitch, I am reminded of finding her facedown and floating, of pulling her from the water and pounding her chest until, sputtering, she came back.

"Sarah," I say, but she's already rolling to her feet, collecting her jeans from beneath the window frame and pulling the legs right side out.

"You ought to go," she says.

I pass her socks from beneath the covers. "Come with me. Just for a while."

"No time for that now."

Bill, her husband, will be an hour yet—gone for supplies. Even after his affair with Daisy-Come-Again, Sarah will stay. Maybe because of the affair, she will stay. She picks at her hair, correcting yellow strays, tucking them behind her ear. She applies her makeup with a hard, pecking hand.

I retrieve my shirt from between the pillows, my hat from the floor.

Bill's mother glares from her portrait on the dresser, gold-rimmed glasses high on her nose, wide as a snorkeling mask.

"Help me make the bed," Sarah says. "Then clear out."

***

I duck into the woods and listen to the helicopters sweep the house. Then I'm threading through the wild pines crowding the little slope that runs to the highway. My truck is hidden in the thick of them. There's gritty bird shit on the windshield and needles piled on the hood.

On the long straight of Luther Street, I can see Bill's truck coming a mile off, and I know he sees mine. We roll on, arms hung out the window like knights in a tilt, fingers flexing in the wind or else tight in a fist. Bill's truck stops level with mine.

"You got a bathing suit?" Bill asks.

"Hm?"

"A bathing suit," he says again.

"What?"

I leave him with that.

Bill's a dentist for money and a carpenter for fun. He's added a two-hundred-square-foot sunroom to his house. The walls are plate glass under crown molding and pine. Sarah's filled the place with peace lilies and indoor palms.

If not for Sarah, I'd welcome the flood that's coming to tear through Issock and bury it under a hundred tons of silt. The glass walls of Bill's house will shatter. The plants will drown. Fish will hang in clouds beneath the cathedral ceiling and drift to the kitchen. Freshwater clams will nestle in the foyer. Maybe an eel will sleep in the bed.

Though, to hear Bill tell it, none of that will happen, and his house, the pride of Baddock County, will float.

Bill Selmy is well-connected. He's done a root canal for the mayor, dug a cellar for the chief of police. When the judge's wife knocked out all her teeth ice-skating, Bill screwed in a set of porcelain veneers. He built the town a gazebo in the park with the names of every war veteran posted around the roof in hammered brass, six Selmy men among them. And because Bill says the pontoons he's installed beneath the foundations of his house will float the whole towering mess of it above the flood, people believe him.

The media ran with it. News crews drove out to hear Bill explain how the wedge-nosed pontoons—"like the prow of a ship!"—will part the waters of soon-to-be Lake Issock and lift his house high above their heads. Experts were dispatched. Measurements were taken. And when the right heads had nodded and the right papers were signed, Bill was granted his floating castle along with limited rights to the lake, should his house survive.

Three hours before the flood, I'm lying on my back across a table in the 1-2-Diner and chewing one plastic straw after another until they're nothing but flattened shreds. The town is all but empty, and the tornado sirens are going off every ten minutes for the holdouts to flee. The only cars on the road are the deputy sheriffs', but the diner is dead and I'm parked out back, so they don't bother me. I smell meat patties rotting. The sun cuts through the split blinds and warms my eyelids. I've settled to die.

The door jingles, and Roe Freeman, the sheriff proper, comes to hover over my table. His gut blots out the light of day.

"Diner's closed," he says.

"Curl up and die."

"I've got some chicken," he says, and sits down with a box. "Set them wifey woes aside and share some chicken with your brother."

It was his ease and appetite that made him my mother's favorite.

"Time was, she'd have left with me," I say.

"Time was never."

"If I had asked last year. After the affair," I say. I fish in the box of bones. The breasts, thighs, and legs have been picked clean. I take a wing.

"But you didn't ask her."

I shake my head. "I just didn't ask right."

When Roe was in diapers, Sarah and I were fogging up my mother's Malibu. There's something special in those initial fumblings that he can't understand. A sacred trust, like love for the self—something. Roe's great love was a horse named Betty's Thigh that won him a Pick 6. Sarah and I married the week after the race and divorced before the winnings were spent.

After Sarah found Bill in his office, the patient chair reclined and Daisy-Come-Again white-knuckling the headrest, she stayed with me for a month or so. She left when I proposed again. That was my mistake.

"Camera on one of those hello-copters saw you leaving her house," Roe says. He makes a buttermilk biscuit disappear in two bites.

"I can't say goodbye?"

"That what you were saying?"

I turn my hand into a bird, and outside the flood sirens wail.

"Yeah." Roe wipes his hands on the drapes. Then he puts three rounds from his .38 into the back of the cash register.

I roll onto the floor and listen to Roe belly laughing. He passes me his baton and, because I know he means well, I let into the cake display first and the framed poster of the "So Sweet Apple Pie" after that. We trash the stools and the countertop, and for a minute all memory recedes, but then Roe starts ripping off the tops of the tables and it comes back: Sarah serving coffee and pie to the out-of-towners while I turned sausage at all hours of the night. Some nights there'd be no one but us. We'd pass maraschino cherries mouth to mouth over the counter.

Roe gets his hands on a broomstick and chants for a pitcher.

I line up across the floor and start whizzing mugs into the tile wall while Roe heaves the broom. High. High. Low. I lob one underhand, and he connects, bellowing like an ape.

Roe sits down. His tan sheriff's shirt is soaked through. "Better?" he asks.

"Yeah."

In the parking lot, my truck is nowhere to be seen.

"You'll find it at Showman," Roe says, and waits for me to walk to his squad car. "You drive," he says, and when I climb into the cab, he handcuffs me to the wheel. It's his party trick.

The Crown Vic lumbers up to speed while the AM radio garbles about Bill's house and history in the making. The birds, I see, are flitting from tree to tree and calling out. I've read that before floods, hurricanes, even tornados, stampedes of wild animals can predict disaster. I imagine the unnatural surge of the water pulling birds from the air and consider that the ground will fill first and how great the unending bulk of the new lake will feel above the centipedes and moles—the crushing weight of it driving them deeper then snuffing them out.

Between the low, brick buildings of town, what cars weren't worth the move line the streets. Clunkers mostly, of which there are a herd in Issock—hand-me-down Civics with crushed-in bumpers and trucks sitting on two or more donuts with their tailgates broken off.

I'm surprised to see Spaceman Howl's Buick parked outside the boarded-up drugstore. His Shepherd bitch, Molly, sits in the passenger seat. In his youth, Spaceman was a pilot of jets. Because he was said to have shot down several enemy planes, he became briefly famous. It came out eventually that Spaceman had actually spent his years in the service coiling hose on an aircraft carrier, but not before he capitalized on his fame by way of a fairly lucrative pool-digging service—a venture I joined him in. It was shit work and long days driving a Bobcat, shoving around the dirt that Spaceman would scoop out of folk's backyards, but I had a family, and it got me out of the diner.

The first pool I dug for Spaceman was my own, which seemed like a big idea at the time. It had a shallow end that stretched for ten yards and faded down to nothing, so the water met your toes like waves on a beach. I cut a deep end fifteen feet down and set a spring board overtop; in school, Sarah was a diver.

We were proud. I had one of Roe's deputies make me an oil drum smoker that would cook five chickens end to end. We had people over for drinking and tooling around. Everybody'd bring their kids and dogs. Our boy, Harlan, was easy to spot. Only three, but a head of strawberry curls to shame Shirley Temple.

Things got comfortable. We had a pile of friends. The drinking got a little out of hand, for Sarah and me. I woke in the middle of the night once, Sarah and I stretched out in a lawn chair made for one, covered in morning dew. Friends of ours, the Beesons, had taken Harlan for the night. We had a good laugh about it the next day. A week later, Sarah and I came to under similar circumstances, but the Beesons were out of town. We ran crazy for a few hours after that, looking for the boy. I was going door to door with Roe when Sarah found his body behind the pool ladder.

Spaceman stumbles out from the pharmacy, holding a few plastic bags, and shades his eyes to see who's rolling down the street.

I've got the window down, so it's no trouble to spit.

***

The deputy sheriffs are reporting "all clear" through the radio in Roe's cruiser. They're pulling back to Showman's Hill, a swell of granite like the top of a bald man's head. Its gray rise peeks above the clay and pines and provides a vista. People abandon unwanted animals there to the extent that other people leave food. Over time, a good-sized pack has formed, its members ranging from Tom Ellison's unwanted litter of Dobermans to my own aunt's aging Maltese. Elsewise, it's a decent place to take a girl.

The deputies are excited and chattering about the flood. They've set up a viewing party at Showman's with picnic tables of sweet tea and chicken. Two deputies are already there, fending off the circling pack.

Deputy Watson asks Deputy McCain if he's brought cans or a keg. Deputy Clarke has found paper plates at the Save-A-Lot. No one, it is discovered, remembered ice.

A watermelon rolls at Roe's feet on the passenger's side, and behind the steel cage that bisects the cab, I see gallon jugs of tea jiggling alongside baked mac and cheese. The smell is intoxicating.

We pass Bill's house, and I can see him outside. Sarah is on the porch in a fringe coat. She'll be wearing Western boots underneath.

I suck my teeth.

"Deal with it," Roe says. "Her choice."

"That's nice," I say.

A group of strays crowds in the road ahead, chasing and nipping and otherwise grabbing ass. Some are spotted and a few are black.

We get closer, and the features of the dogs begin to sharpen. A Jack Russell has a limp. A black mutt chomps a ball. Most are deer dogs with tagless orange collars—the kind that sometimes get lost on big hunts. The county leaves boxes for them on the side of the road. I wonder if there are any locked up in the boxes now, padding around in circles and waiting to drown.

Bill's lab, Frank, emerges from the pack and steps into the road, barking and wagging his tail.

I hit the brakes, and a gallon of tea kicks the back of my seat.

Frank shows a toothy grin. *School's out for summer.*

"Pull around him," Roe says.

I putt around to the left, but Frank steps in the way again.

"Hell," Roe says. He reaches over and honks the horn. Nothing happens, and he honks again.

Frank stands to lay his paws on the hood of the car and barks some more. He stares through the glass. *School's out forever.*

"Ho!" A man calls from behind us.

I look into the rearview. It's Bill, jogging up to the cruiser waving his arms over his head like he's signaling a rescue plane.

"Appreciate it," he says, holding Frank by the collar. "Roe. Johnny."

Everyone in town calls me J-Hook except Sarah and, unfortunately, Bill. I've always suspected he did it for spite.

"You got all the animals loaded up in that house, Bill?" Roe asks. "Two by two?"

Bill laughs well. That's his best feature, Sarah says: his laugh. His jolly fucking laugh. He leans in to rest his hands on the windowsill of the cruiser so that he's about a foot from my face. "Just the ones

I like," he says.

"What are you still doing down here, Johnny?" Bill asks.

"Dog catching," I say and regret it because it makes Bill laugh again.

"We've got room in the back yet," Roe says. "Get you and Sarah and the dog in here."

"No, no," Bill says. "This is the real deal."

"Mhm."

In order to smile wider, Bill has to actually open his mouth. "Ah," he says.

Frank's ears perk up, and he takes off running, ripping, to my delight, his collar from Bill's hairy fist.

We all turn to see Sarah walking out of the pines and into the road, pushing Frank down when he jumps.

"Bill," she calls.

"Ayuh," Bill says, and taps the roof of the cruiser. "You boys get out safe."

It occurs to me, as I watch Sarah standing by the roadside, that she is not afraid. She is impatient—ready to be off. She is not spinning her ring the way she used to. She is not pulling at her collarbones the way she did when she was in a stew, or waiting for a phone call. She is not that ashen woman I knew to sit kneading her scalp in the bathtub before a trip to the grocery store.

She looks fine. She is practically glowing, waving at Roe's cruiser while she waits for Bill and now walking away with her hand stuck in the butt pocket of Bill's jeans. She won't know I'm in the car if I don't say something. She'll walk back to Bill's house to have a screw or pet her dog or, otherwise, wait to die.

"You got any ice?" I call out the window to Bill.

"The hell?" Roe asks.

But obliging Bill is already waving us on to where his driveway opens into the main road, and Sarah, I see, has removed her hand from Bill's back pocket and made it into a slender pink hook, like Barrel of Monkeys, and she's hanging it on the ledge of her collarbone. And she is, I know, troubled by the thought that she need not resign herself to this—that I might not allow it, that I am in Roe's cruiser, and that I am still here.

***

"You gonna stop this flood?" Sarah asks from the across her kitchen counter.

Roe and Bill are in the garage filling a cooler with ice.

"Where were you?" my mother asked Sarah at Harlan's wake. She never asked me, then or in the bitter years after. Not even when it was Sarah floating in the pool.

"Why are you doing this?" I ask.

"It's going to be a whole new place after the water comes," she says.

Sarah stretches her arms over the granite. The branching veins make her pearly skin match the stone.

"Just gonna be clean, flat water. Not even gonna be any fish in the place for a few years. That's where I want to live."

"We can leave here just fine," I say. "Don't need a flood for that."

"I want it, Johnny," she said. "To see it buried."

When Bill is away and Sarah calls me—I know it's to go back to the old times. To travel with her eyes squeezed shut and her hands against my back. She wants adolescent fingers on her skin. She wants to be folded in my mother's backseat. She wants the skinny fry cook inside of the diner waitress and the pool digger inside of the woman sunning in her front yard. She wants anything besides the poor, sad mother and father with the dead little boy. She'd drown to forget it, to wash it all away. She'll drown again.

"You ever thought of what'll happen to Harlan?" I ask. "When the water comes."

"That's a rotten thing to say."

"I've been thinking about it."

"Can't see what good that does," she says as she wipes the

counter clean of lunch crumbs.

A helicopter flies low over the house, and the silverware chatters in its drawer.

I see a mouse running along the wall behind Sarah's back. It's got a big wad of something stuffed in its mouth, and it's standing up to paw at the glass walls and doors—looking for a way out.

"Well, I've been thinking about it, and Roe and I moved him."

"Jesus, Johnny."

"I didn't open the box, but—"

"Jesus."

"He'll be up behind Showman's, where he won't get washed out. Should stay above the water."

"You shouldn't have done that," Sarah says. "Shouldn't move a body."

"It's a good place."

The sirens kick on again and it's their swan song, high and sharp.

"Let me show you where."

"Not a church?"

"It's better than a church," I say. "There's a row of azaleas. There's a great big poplar. All those friendly strays stay up there and watch over the place."

There's a part of me that hates to bring Harlan into this, to even say his name. He was here for just a little time, when Spaceman and I were selling pools as fast as we could dig them, and the money was rushing in. I had Sarah quit the diner as soon as we knew there'd be a kid, and she grew distant, obsessed with making ready, with buying this and that, with rearranging and babyproofing the house.

When the boy came, I took as many jobs from Spaceman as I could. I packed lunch and dinner. I worked under electric lights and came home well into the night. And when the boy died, for me, it was like he was never there. There was always a place where he might have been; a gouged-out hole. But it was Sarah I missed. It was my wife.

"Let me show you," I say.

Bill and Roe come into the kitchen.

"Let's go," Roe says.

"I'm asking Sarah if she'll come pay her respects," I say.

"Respects to who?" Bill asks.

Roe hooks my arm and pulls me toward the door where the mouse is still looking for a way out.

"To Harlan. He's been reburied. She should see where."

Sarah finds something to pick at in the sink.

"Flood's in an hour or less," Bill says.

"I'll take her back in a boat. Or a submarine."

"No," Sarah says, and leaves the room.

Bill isn't laughing now. "I think you'd better go," he says. "There'll be time for that later. If she wants."

It occurs to me that I've never really looked at Bill in the face. He looks old. He's well-muscled and taller than me by a head. The skin around his eyes is raccoon-tanned from his sunglasses. He could be mayor. He could have a different Daisy-Come-Again every week. What makes a man like that want to drown on national TV? What makes a man like that want my wife?

Bill puts his paw of a hand on my shoulder and leads me, with Roe's help, to the big glass door of his house.

Outside, Frank is barking and snarling at the helicopter over the house. The air is humming with the noise of sirens and engines and wind. The little trees are bending where they stand.

"You'll kill her," I say.

"No," Bill says. "I won't."

Roe pulls me down the driveway. Beneath Bill's house, the pontoons stand in long lines, their steel noses upturned. There are dozens of them, and they look tiny. Miniscule. They cover the house's belly like the legs of a millipede.

I imagine the waves, great white waves, atomic bomb waves, rolling down the cleared and waiting street. I see them blowing Bill's truck away, throwing it like a toy. The skinny pines are fodder. I see the trees and the truck and the water colliding with the pontoons, swallowing the house whole. The floats break and race away. Their silver backs breach the surface. From Showman's, the deputy sheriffs point like whale watchers on a pleasure cruise.

Sarah looks down on me from her bedroom window. The blood in her face has drained away. Her eyes are red. She looks like the girl I married, and she looks like a ghoul.

A voice comes from the helicopter, deafening and robotic. "Clear the area."

I wave off the pilot and slip into the cruiser. Before Roe can get to his side, I've got the old girl in gear and whining, back, back down the driveway and now on, on toward Bill's house. The pedal is hard against the floor, and Roe is beside the road, waving like a madman for me to "Stop! STOP!"

But the cruiser is hungry for the pontoons. She wants to taste their silver flesh. She wants to plow into them and tear through their papery tin skin, one after the next, all the way down the line. She wants to be my voice when I say, one more time, "Please. Don't wash away."

THE WAR OF NAKED AGGRESSION

The stool in Westmore Community Art Center was cold. It had chilled in the night air, the windows left open for the mild Georgia winter to creep through the hall and pool in the studios—the preference of the county's janitorial brigade. Anders sat, hunched and naked, in Studio C before a dozen seniors, technical school professors, and housewives. On the stool next to him was a new model: one Rose C. Lee.

Before last week's class, Westmore's director, Kyiah, had scheduled a meeting with both Rose and Anders, introducing them and letting Anders know that Rose would be modeling for the classes now as well, but that the funding allotted for models would remain the same, as would the class times. They would share.

Rose had looked lesser in her clothes, Anders thought. A short woman in paint-smeared jeans and a shirt with the neck stretched out. Hair and eyes an unremarkable brown. She slouched in Kyiah's pleather chair, hands in her jacket pockets. She chewed gum. These were not the gestures that one longed for later. Things missed if not drawn out.

"I think this is a change for the better. The best possible thing," Kyiah said, clasping hands over a herringbone skirt. "A man and a woman. A woman and a man. How complete for the class." Though, when Anders thought of Rose standing next to him in Studio C, he did not imagine them in harmony, standing like Genesis with fig leaves and forest animals and their hair blown out; he could only imagine invasion.

In the hallway, after the meeting, Anders gave Rose the names of several other community centers and studio spaces in bordering counties. "You won't much like these geezers here," he said. "All old. Not very skilled. And the pay." Anders made a thumbs-down.

"I think I'll stay on," Rose said.

"Well, it would be best to split the classes by day," he said. "You can start with Sundays."

"That works," Rose said. "And the Tuesday/Thursday classes as well. I'll be at those."

Rose stayed to observe Anders' session that day. She sat with a straight back in a folding chair and doodled with a ballpoint and didn't say much as the geezers sketched and Anders moved through his usual forms. All of Studio C was invited for post-session wine at the town bistro or the house of one of the geezers. Rose came along to familiarize herself with the group. "It's not Lee like 'Robert E.,'" she clarified.

Anders scoffed. "Where do you come from?" he asked, but no one seemed to hear.

"Lee like an island," Rose said. "Leeward. Away from the storm."

Several geezers moaned affirmations, or else bobbed their heads slowly, or else crowed from the table head for her to "say again!?"

Her wine glass still full, Rose cleaned her teeth with a napkin edge. She was new, Anders thought. Why shouldn't she fuss over her teeth? She was a transplant come down from Iowa or Idaho or some place. She was new and Anders was king here, and as such, he could welcome her with ease. One touch of his hand, one kindly smirk, and she would be accepted. She would be whole. And when the weight of the crown shifted against her, when she felt unloved and unstudied next to him, he would make her understand that Sundays were where she should live. The weekday classes were his domain. He would get to sleep in on the weekends, and things would be fine.

Anders reached across the table, his hand appearing before him as the marble palm of David, if hairier. Open with fingers slightly bent. He sensed the table of novices lean in to glimpse the powerful swell of his thumb, the wise tracks set into the palm; if their eyes were sharper, they might have seen the colored suggestions of veins. He looked at Rose meaningfully, in olive branch and broken bread. He wished he had a ring, that she might press it to her lips. "We're glad to have you," he said.

Rose stood from the table. She touched her palm to her chin and turned her head slowly from side to side, then she shook out her arms like a fighter. The geezers were transfixed. "Where's the john?" Rose asked.

"Back left," Anders said, but she was already gone.

"I much prefer your lips," Phyllis said next to him. She had gone to school with Anders' mother. "So angular."

Phyllis was drawing a fried egg into her napkin. No, an oyster. Anders recognized the murky reflection of his own left ear and sucked in his breath. He laid his hand over his ear and leaned against it, as if bored.

"Your lines were crude today," he said without looking at Phyllis, and the old woman wilted away.

At the next session, a steel rivet pressed through the meat of Anders' right buttock, like a finger jabbing to the bone. He was in his Thinker pose and had been holding a half-crunch for twenty minutes. His muscles ached, but the muted scraping of a dozen pencils serenaded him. It was his metronome and balm, the unifying cadence when his joints begged for reprieve. It was the sound of being remembered. The sound that accompanied the airy mass of rheumy eyes flying about his every surface. It almost tickled, the eyes landing and flitting back to their pad and then lighting on his skin again. Except, it wasn't all the eyes. He could feel it: the absence of adoration. A syphoning of ambrosia.

Rose sat with her chest thrust out and her arms locked behind. Her legs were crossed at the ankles and outstretched, so her long muscles perked to glow in the naked, overhead light. Her triceps and shoulders stood rocky, and there was a marvel in the way her veins buried and unearthed themselves—appearing, just beneath the skin, as the splintering of a river across her shoulder before resurfacing over bands of muscle in the bicep, the forearm, the bulges of the hand where it gripped the lip of the stool. What had she done to earn veins like that? Anders imagined her in the dark of morning, hoisting bags of cement with a pulley and chain. Deadlifting truck axles. Drinking eggs from a pitcher of stone, a hollowed skull.

Anders watched the right side of the room, those geezers more directly in front of Rose were absorbed in the worship of her knees—the charm of the patella above the lacing quadriceps with the true line of the shin. A bead of sweat rolled from the shadow of Rose's armpit and cut a path to her waist. When Anders looked back to Rose's face, he saw that she was watching him. He shifted his eyes to the crowd of seats and saw that they were all watching her then. Every one of them, turning for fresh sheets. They put away their half-finished pages of Anders and began new pages of Rose.

"Pose shift," Anders said, and stretched his back. He took a wooden dowel from his bin of materials and turned at the waist while he gripped it, stretching and eventually freezing in a left-facing trunk-twist, his legs spread in an athletic stance. His eyes looked out into the high-nowhere of the room, finding the familiar corner where a spider had lived and died and now shriveled in its own silken mausoleum. The Modern Man, this pose was called.

Rose's arms reached beneath Anders' to clasp over his chest. They were heavy. The fingers were calloused. Her breath smelled of cigarettes. "This OK?"

"Of course," Anders said, though he had never posed with a partner before. Murmurs rose from the crowd of artists as materials were readied and exchanged. Chairs scooted about in the constant game of light and eye, each shift revealing a new relief.

Rose matched her feet to Anders'. She mirrored the twist of his spine and drew long, indulgent breaths that made her nipples graze his back. The slight round of her belly rested against his skin. A heat grew where she touched him. He began to sweat.

"Dr. Jervais," Rose commanded, and Claude stood as if trumpeted for. Traitorous Claude, so eager for a new form. "Let's get the big light involved. And cut the overhead here."

Oohs and aahs circulated the room. They didn't often use the spotlight in the corner, an ancient steely thing, rusted from someone's garage.

"That's fine," Anders said, but a few of the geezers were already positioning the spotlight, dragging it, squealing, over the linoleum so that it shown, hot and unblinking, on Anders' shoulders, cooking the wafer of his ear.

Anders knew that the muffled squeaks of the pencil tips, the taps and scrapes of the pens, they must be out there, filling the room, but the humming of the spotlight and the harshness of its beam had made him blind and deaf—marooned. Then the hands around him shifted, and Rose's palm pressed into the hollow of his sternum.

"When Sherman took Savannah," she whispered to his ear. "He left it unburnt." Her head rested below his left shoulder, away from the room of eyes. "That's how I'd like to leave you," she said.

"What?"

"Merry Christmas," Rose said, and nudged the back of Anders' leg with her knee. His weight shifted, falling on the heel of his right foot and stinging under the load. "Sherman gave the city for a gift."

"I know," he said. "Everyone knows that."

"What was that?" Phyllis asked from somewhere in the room.

"Maintain focus," Anders called out.

"I'm Sherman," Rose said. "And Lincoln. We're the Union, these old folks and me."

"I'm Savannah?" Anders asked through the corner of his lips.

"You lived in Savannah. You're like. . ." Rose let her head rest on the high of Anders' back, on the trapezius he had lovingly, daily, hardened and stretched that it might peek, just so, above his shoulder. She sighed. "You're like a man. In Savannah. A statue of a man. You don't live there anymore."

"Why are you here?"

"This is my work," she said. "I'm good at it."

"But why are you *here*?"

"The weather's fine. Kyiah's a friend. And the museum gig, of course. Long term."

Kyiah, Anders thought. Of course, Kyiah. Kyiah, who worked part-time at the art center and part-time for the historical society. Kyiah, who had never once invited him to model in the traveling "Life-Size Civil War" dioramas put on monthly. There had been hints she might try to be rid of him—unexpected drop-ins during sessions and long, meandering meetings afterwards, making him late for wine socials and bistro dinners on the geezer's dime.

Kyiah wanted something from him. Something "universal." Anders wasn't sure what that meant. There was a universal quality to his body. His body that was *like* any body. His body that could be anybody or anything, when viewed in the correct light. The arc of his back might well be the Knife Edge summit of Mount Katahdin. The dip and dark of his navel, the shadow of areola before the rocky stud of his nipple; these were universal. They might be the pits and shadows of the moon. The poses he employed were meant to be all of these things. All of these and more. He had explained this to Kyiah, who only nodded over her tea.

"You've been here, what? A week?" Anders whispered. "I've been running this for two years. People have come. People have died. I'm on refrigerators. Living rooms. Bathrooms. The women, their husbands are gone. It's me over their beds."

"Kyiah said you do the same three poses every class. She said there've been complaints."

"Bull."

"If it were bull, Kyiah wouldn't have called."

"Hold still please!" Mrs. Orbee called from the back of the room. Anders and Rose straightened some.

"You're going to get a phone call," Rose said. "I give it a week. Maybe less."

Sweat ran freely down Anders' back where Rose clung, content. He squinted out to see where the spider web was, but it was lost. What was out there for him if Rose was right? Not much. There was his day job, serving lunch at the state's Home for Veterans, changing the trash bins and playing the geezers in checkers and walking them to and from their beds. There were the other venues he'd told Rose about, underfunded or extinct. Anders had visited them all and sat alone in his robe more than once. This was where the eyes were. This was his little slice of fame, and if it was nothing, what of it? In the grand scheme of things, it was all nothing. If the bombs dropped tomorrow and the world were mostly ash, it would all be nothing. Let him die, at least, with his love of self intact, knowing that he was beloved in the way the amoeba under the microscope is beloved—in that he was studied and picked from the millions and billions by way of his occupying the lens and that his all-in-all was relished and repeated in parts and in wholes.

And if the bombs stayed asleep, resting in their bunkers and warehouses and hanger bays, what then? A generation lives; a generation dies. But the portraits of Anders, the many, many portraits of Anders, those lived on. Those were put behind glass. Those were rolled and stowed in an attic box that would one day be given to a child and put in their attic and then another attic and then, one day, when hovercrafts buzz the sky and parents customize their children like pizzas from their phones, portraits of Anders will be rolled out again. "Look! Jesus, look!" They will say in the future. "Here is a man!" And in the way that all art is prized, if old enough or foreign enough or related to the finder in some way, Anders will be prized. Even the Anders that lives and comes to life through the sluggish hand of the dotard Phyllis will be prized. And, the fact was, this is where the dotards lived. This is where the dotards sketched. This is where he must be.

"Pose shift," he said, and broke from Rose's arms. The cold air of the studio dried his sweat and prickled his skin. If there had been complaints, the geezers were complicit in this. For all Anders knew, they had their calendars marked. Had invited Rose over for lunch and ridden together to her first session. Anders eyed them now, scuttling and adjusting and waiting for him, who had for so long been the light of their Tuesday and Thursday evenings, to decide on a pose. Doubtless, they were expecting Ascension, wherein he stood like Christ in the center of the room, with his legs together and his arms outstretched and his face inclined to the fluorescent lights like: "Father, forgive these backwards, yokel geezers and their frail attempts to capture me on their pulp sheets." It was a favorite, but today he crouched, head and arms down like a sprinter. "Sixty seconds," Anders chimed, and the pencils raced. From between his legs, he watched Rose mount her stool and sit with her hands on her leg, as if massaging a knot from the muscle.

"When Sherman took Atlanta. When he shelled and burned it. He spared Newnan." Anders said. "It's a little bedroom town."

"I know," Rose said.

"Well, do you know what happened after he left it?"

"He marched to the ocean. Took Savannah. Crushed the heartland. Named his horses Dolly, Duke, and Sam."

"Yes," Anders said. The clock on the wall hadn't made a circuit yet, but he wanted to move. "Pose shift," he said, and walked out of the spotlight to stand in the center of the room and assume Ascension, his reflection foggy in the buffed, gray tile beneath him. The room of geezers surrounded him, and he was, again, the sun. He was of solar importance. Anything that lived behind the geezers's eyes and squeezed out onto their page, it was all his energy passing from one form to the next. In the way the farmer trades the corn to the mother who makes the child who grows the corn are only passing and passing back the same bunch of joules—so too were the geezers making and trading and being Anders on their pages and in their minds. In their very brains and blood was Anders: their all-in-all.

"When Sherman left, the rest of Atlanta came to Newnan," he said. "They looked at the beauty of the buildings Sherman and his armies had left, and they knew it was Sherman's vanity that saved them—because he wanted it for himself. The wraparound porches and pink azalea hedges and the brassy-red railcars on the streets."

"It was worth keeping," Rose said.

"It was worth stealing. But when Sherman left and the people of Atlanta got out to Newnan and saw what Sherman wanted—" Anders lies down on the floor with the big florescent lights over him and made an angel with his arms. "Pose shift," he cooed to the geezers.

"When they saw Newnan, they burned it themselves."

"Belligerent," Rose said.

"And powerful," Anders looked down lovingly at his body, his arms at his sides now and the length of him curling like a fish on the floor, offered up to the geezers to be made permanent. He watched them, bent like monks over vellum, quills loaded with the blood of the lamb.

"And vain," Rose said.

"But it was their vanity over his. They would rather the whole thing go than have it taken because, really, all the parts of it that were essential couldn't be burned—not by Sherman. If Georgia burns by Georgian hands, the memory is one of sacrifice, not conquest. It's spit-in-the-eye, not a loss."

"You gonna spit in my eye?" Rose asked from her stool. Her toes were fanned out before her so the light made little shadows between each one, like stages of the moon. Why hadn't Anders ever thought of that?

"No," he said, and then laid still on the floor to consider the lies he had been spinning and where, if not here, he might live and be drawn. He reached out to the blurry lines of Westmore County in his mind and felt around them for some secret commune of mediocre artists, and he strained to think of another way to go about the work of becoming immortal. There were pools of marsh mud that dried and hardened to make a sort of cement, and if the course of the salt river shifted and the tide line moved, those cracked stretches of earth might remain. He could go to the tidal muds and make presses of his chest and hands, his back and buttocks—two shallow divots to live and breathe for him when he was gone and mutants walk the earth. There wasn't much else that he could imagine.

Anders stood from the floor. He brushed the dust and eraser shreds and stray hairs from his arms. "Time," he said, but the geezers kept working.

Rose hadn't moved from her pose on the stool.

"Time," he said again, but no one budged. They were transfixed. Locked in the study of Rose's toes, which she arrayed like a hand of cards. "That's it!" he shouted. Possibly they had all died and were stuck in some sort of joint nerve twitch. Perhaps the bombs had dropped, and this was the fever afterwise that would last until the dead rise to say His name. Perhaps, perhaps.

"A few minutes more?" Rose asked, and the geezers murmured in agreement.

Anders walked the room, looking at the easels and sketchbooks. On them: Rose's back. Her spine, a mountain road. Stars and cirrus clouds for freckles and scars. Flower blossoms for ears. Phyllis's study of Rose's hands, with only the wispy afterthoughts of his chest hair beneath them to highlight the edge of her knuckle. Maxwell's reflection of Rose's breasts. Claude's good black ink poured over Rose's shoulders, the impossible line of the triceps where it fused stool to hand to arm to back. And nowhere was Anders. Anders was gone.

Rose called, "Time." She unballed a terry cloth robe from the corner of the room and slipped it on while the geezers shuffled out.

Anders sat on the windowsill and felt the night's first breaths slide past his hips. "I don't understand," he said.

"That's not bad," Rose said. From the door of the studio, she took a picture of him with her phone, naked behind the sea of empty easels and desks. "When Sherman sent Lincoln the letter that Savannah had been won, you know what it was worth? What the whole city was worth?" The smoke of her cigarette coiled over her head.

"Yes," Anders said.

"250,000 bales of cotton. Dried. Unburned. Packaged and gifted and shipped to Boston to make blue shirts and blue pants and baby clothes and a blanket for someone's horse. It was a job. And nobody died. And the sun went down and the sun came up." She raised her phone again with both hands, her cigarette clenched in her teeth. "Smile."

"That's only half the story," Anders began, imagining heroes with names he hadn't formed yet hiding away secrets from the invaders—sealing them in burlap and skins and sinking them into the Savannah River, maybe with barrels for floats, and they could paint the barrels white and red and pretend they were for guiding ships, and so even when the city was taken and the ships were captured and converted and the people made into subjects, even then, there would be gold under the water and waiting. Maybe still waiting on the bottom of the river now, cleverly packed and dry. All the heroes of Anders' mind were like that: conditionally defeated but never entirely stripped. And so, eventually, when the world had spun ten thousand more times and the remembering had warped and warped again, and the occupiers were gone, and all that remained were old portraits and photographs, and you could shift and change the facts to suit your needs—you could win. It might be portraits of Anders to survive in the self-storage center while Rose's toes burnt with the house. Who says what will last?

But Rose had not stayed for the story, and he was alone in the room of easels now. Outside in the parking lot, the geezers were loading their work into their cars and calling out to one another, arguing about where to sit in the bistro and who the waitress would be and how much she should be tipped.

In the corner of Studio C were clay projects left by Monday's ceramics class, most wrapped and covered in plastic so they wouldn't dry out. Anders pulled back the sheeting to see the chubby-legged horses and too-tubular dolphins and other blobs of the clay tortured into wobbly bowls. One by one, he smashed the pieces into a singular mound, dousing it with water and working the pile to a smoothness before carrying it, wrapped in a towel, to Kyiah's office desk to tender his surrender. Gripping the desk and bending at the waist, he forced his face into the clay. When he was finished, he had made a hole.

VALHALLA, GEORGIA

Crocodiles are easy. People are harder.
–Steve Irwin

In 2006, Steve Irwin was killed by a stingray. *The Telegraph* reports that he was stabbed hundreds of times by an animal roughly six hundred pounds and seven feet across, wing to wing. His cameraman said he passed peacefully, in shock.

In 2011, my father moves to Savannah. I decide to drive down. It is November. We keep the fireplace loaded, but it's too warm to burn the wood. We should be celebrating. Dad has come back from six months of rehabilitation in Jacksonville, where he gave his life to Christ.

Of course, my father says, it's a process. There are setbacks. It may be that he will never have it whipped. Not forever. Religion allows for that. It is understanding. Redemption is a guarantee. And if you ever get a chance at a guarantee, my father says, you take it.

I am a shaman. This is not like a priest who communicates with God regularly and with certain privileges. Receiving a response. And it is not like a faith healer or snake handler who implores God to soothe an arthritic body or allow someone to speak in languages that no living person knows or else make animals calm. This is not even like actual Shamanism. I am a shaman where "shaman" means a person with the right idea. A godly idea, made for a singular purpose.

My purpose is to get my father into heaven. To this end, I have driven from my home in Alabama with three timber rattlesnakes in the backseat of my car, all of them tied in one pillowcase, kept without a meal for two days.

I have been granted a vision of the afterlife. I know how it works. The rich side and the quiet side. I know who goes where.

I believe I was granted this vision because my father and I watched Steve Irwin on television three nights a week and because once, when I was four or five, we fed strips of fried chicken to three alligator whelps we were keeping in our cast-iron tub. My father taped their mouths closed. Told me, "Get behind their ears."

A few years later, we adopted a black racer named Pudge. It was an indoor–outdoor pet that lived, generally, beneath the roots of an oak in our front yard and, occasionally, on our screened porch, where my father and I planted snakes for Pudge to "hunt." Usually garter and rat snakes. We'd stare from the dirt yard outside, crouched with our faces pressed to the screen, watching Pudge strike and coil then inch his enemy down.

The morning I earned my driver's license, my father leapt from our truck, sprinted twenty yards, and dove onto the back of a five-foot alligator. He said it was walking toward the road. He didn't want it to get hit. We fit a dog collar around its neck and tied it to the bumper of my mother's car. It was Mother's Day.

As a child, I knew: heaven was wild. It was made for the wild. Everyone knew animals were wise. That in their silence was an unmatched intimacy with God, the planet, and certain truth. Steve Irwin met the animals in the wild, where he was bitten and stung with extreme presence. The closer a person was to animals, the closer they were to God.

I didn't know what new kind of Jesus my father had signed on with, if not the wild one. When he was on the phone, I had a hard time knowing if he was drunk. I second-guessed my instincts, listening to him talk. I saw him fighting pythons in my sleep, and he spoke to me with a clarity I hadn't heard for years, while the snakes crushed his ribs. I had to drive to see him.

Now he tells me that over 30 percent of alcoholics die alcohol-related deaths. He's watching the muted news while he speaks, slumped down in an easy chair and looking near dead already. I ask him if that isn't like saying most knife fighters die from being stabbed. "This is a disease," he says, "and it may kill me."

Next he tries to give me things. His deer rifle. Some stiff dress shoes. A collection of novels by Louis L'Amour. The only book he reads now is the *Big Book*. I turn it all down.

We watch silent flood footage on the TV set. Men and women in the tops of trees. "That's a mess," my father says.

"Yeah."

For a moment, I'm twelve again and he's working nights. Not coming home until the middle of the day. I don't see him. We don't talk. He leaves infrequent notes on the refrigerator that say, in block letters, I LOVE YOU or DID YOU EAT ALL THE LUNCH FISH? I consider that I have grown callous and unfair. I'm lucky to have him here, sober and with a project. Re-establishing his life. Getting to work regularly. Maybe I should be proud of that. It's just, all my life, he taught me to be proud of something else.

"Go and get us a Coke, son."

I slip out to the car and retrieve the sack of snakes. They're too dazed to strike the cotton anymore. With care, I empty the rattlers into the central hallway of my father's house. They slither toward the living room, apprehensive of the carpeted floor. They know what to do. I've seen it a dozen times.

I walk back to the garage. "Dad," I say. "Help me organize these tools?"

Do I want to kill my father? I want to save him. I want to jar him. After years of watching his decline—admiration turned to confusion to pity to contempt—I want to see him fight with something real. Something scaly. Something that will remind him of who he was. Call that Achilles back from whatever beach. Or kill him. Send his soul to Valhalla, Georgia.

I will thank the timber rattlers and shoo them outside while the cargo lamps of the Valkyries' Dodge pickups light their approach into my father's front yard. I'll cry happy when they drop the tailgate and load him into the bed then putter away to the land of deep woods and crushed oyster shell roads, and men who latch small lizards to their earlobes and noses, and hard fighting monster bass, big as dogs.

"Come on," I say. "I don't know where these tools go." I hear the tortured spring of the easy chair as he stands, walks my way, lumbers into the dark hallway where the snakes are. *Decide,* I think. *Choose to live.*

"Great God!" he shouts. "There's snakes in here! Three snakes."

I hang my head around the corner to see him retreating, crow hopping over the carpet to his kitchen. "What kind are they?" I ask.

"Shit, I don't know."

"Did you check? Where is the light? Maybe they're nothing. Could be garters."

He comes back with a flashlight and shines the snakes, who are rattling sweetly, their brown backs agreeing with the carpet. Blending in. They form three, tight coils. Saying, *Try us. Really, come try.*

"Shit. It's rattlers."

"Seems like it," I say. "Got a stick? We've moved worse."

"Stick nothing," he says. "We ought to call the police. Animal control." He starts checking his kitchen drawers.

"Have you seen my phone?" he asks. I watch him rolling open drawers and then, "Christ!" My father's phone is slammed to the floor. I can see him stomping it to pieces. I wonder how close it came to his neck. How high he lifted the phone before he saw the brown recluse clinging to the case. A spider no bigger than a quarter but able to send him to the higher plane to join Steve Irwin, wrestling alligators forever, nose-striking bull sharks, stalking misty valleys with every caveman killed by mammoth tusk.

Without belief in luck, I found the spider in the garage yesterday.

It had fuzzy mandibles and a body the color of a pecan. Once, my father captured four in one day. We kept them alive and in separate jars at my school's Nature Fair. We labeled our display *King Killers*, after the folk legend that Native Americans slipped the spiders into baskets of maize they were forced to cede to British colonists. A bite on the hand might take the whole arm.

"What is it?"

"Fucking spider."

"Did it bite you?"

"No. My phone is wrecked. Call the police."

"My phone's dead," I say. "Here." I toss an oak limb over the snake pile. I chose it for the L-bend at its end. The perfect tool for pressing the neck of a snake to the ground. "Get them with that."

"Why don't you do it?"

"I don't know how," I say.

My father leaves the stick on the floor and does a little panic dance while the snakes crawl toward the kitchen. Snake Raphael and Snake Michael. And this one here, stretching out toward my father's bare feet, he is like Milton's Abdiel, who, though he was the least of the angels, struck Satan across the brow with a spear. Knocked him on his ass. I'm praying: Go on, little Abdiel. Go!

But Dad tears open the rolltop breadbox. I didn't know he kept a handgun in the kitchen.

"Stay in the garage," he calls, and starts in on the rattlers, the gun deafening in the house, a sharp ringing fills my ears. The bullets score the floor. One puts a hole through the drywall when it bounces off the concrete floor. My father clips the heads from three snakes in five shots.

For the first time in shaman-hood, I am at a loss. I don't know what to do. Maybe I had done enough.

"Christ's sake."

I collect the busted snakes from the floor. "You want me to save the rattles?" I ask. He's breathing heavy, leaning on the kitchen counter. Says, "No, Son, no."

***

When Steve Irwin died, I was already out of the house. My father was separated from my mother, living alone in a slouchy, tin-roofed place next to the peanut factory across town. That didn't stop him from stumbling around her front yard at odd hours, picking up sticks and shed palm fronds until the deputy sheriff arrived. He had already tried to kill himself by driving his truck into a municipal dumpster, though, he said after, he had only fallen asleep at the wheel.

Soon after the accident, he called me. I was at a party in Atlanta and stepped outside. "I love you," he said. His voice was shaky. Weepy. "I love you, too," I said. There didn't seem to be anything else coming. No other sentiment. He hung up soon after but called back a week later, sounding worse, to say the same. I figured it was just a matter of time before he ended it. Maybe that sounds hard-hearted. What could I say?

"Steve Irwin died," I told him the next time he called.

"Had it coming," my father said. "That guy was a nut."

That's when the python dreams started. The snakes started hardening themselves into points in my head. I started to relive the old times with the alligators and the raccoons and all the other crawlies. I think it was because I wanted to understand. Clairvoyance.

When Steve Irwin left the world, it was like he dragged a film from over it, and I could see the connections between man and myth. I saw the loving contest of a man leaping onto a saltwater crocodile—for love. This is not a perfect union of understanding. Steve Irwin cannot talk with the animals, but he can rely on them. He can rely on their actions to be sincere. He can be sure that the animal wants to live. It was his joy to observe this will. In being near it, I believe it solidified his own will to live. To grow, to educate, to be thrilled.

Today, my father and I are cramped into a booth at the grocery store. We are eating fried chicken wings, green beans, mashed potatoes and brown gravy. "I mean, can you believe that?" he says. "Can you believe any of that?" He holds his hand up, makes the shape of a gun. "I mean I just dropped the sights down on them," he says. "Pow."

There's some life in him. It's more than I've seen in a while, but I'm not convinced. When I was young, he would have considered it cowardly to kill a snake—anything less than a diamondback. Now he's celebrating. So excited. He's spitting food across the table. He's bearing down too hard with his fork and knife, sawing through the Styrofoam lunch tray.

"You didn't have to shoot them," I say. "You could have used the stick."

"There were three rattlesnakes in the house, and you threw me a stick. Does that make any sense to you?"

"What about Pudge?" I say. "You caught him with your bare hands."

"That was different. Nonvenomous."

"I'm just saying, you never shot them before."

"Well, I didn't see you jumping in," he says. "I don't know what I'll do about my phone. I have to call my sponsor."

I didn't think about that. About that sort of recovery. I was thinking of death or glory. I was thinking of him bleeding a stop-and-go fountain from his foot, cut while we fought a storm on St. Catherines Sound. Nose to the waves, the wild rise and brutal fall. The cooler smashed and the boat's deck sliding in blood and ice and bass and flounder. I don't know how we made it home except he willed it so.

I have spring-boarded off my father's example. Off his wages. I have gone to college and I have become someone who would probably not know my father, even when he was at his best. Even when he was catching peacocks with cast nets. Even when he was taking me trapping. We were selling raccoons so I could go to Kennedy Space Center on an overnight field trip. I never asked if that humiliated him or if he was having as much fun as me, getting up early and drinking black coffee, checking the cages in secret places that only we knew. We let the possoms and stray cats and foxes go free, but hefted, like trophies, the fat, forty-dollar raccoons.

But now I see him, red-eyed over his chicken wings because we don't have much to say to each other anymore, and I get red-eyed over mine, and I remember what a girlfriend of mine said after the Atlanta party call when I was praying he'd wander off like a dog and die. She said love doesn't always look the same, year after year. It requires more of us as we age. It's not the freely given, all-forgiving thing it used to be.

I am a shaman, and I have learned that love, and only love, can save us from the hell that's coming. Love of bravery and goodness and things with sharp teeth. Heaven is wild, and you can't go if you let your mistakes crush you under a bottle or in a car or quietly on the end of a telephone line with nothing to report but the day's work.

"Come on," I say. "Let's go home."

***

We pull into the front yard, and I start walking.

"Where are you going?" he asks.

"Come on and see this," I say. "I see something moving." I hop the fence girding the backyard, but he stays on the other side.

In the depths of the backyard, I lift the little brown tarp I stowed the animal under. A three-foot alligator thrashes left to right. It's terrified, hissing and backed up against a skinny pine. There is no electrical tape holding this alligator's mouth closed. Not anymore. Like a miracle, it appeared to me beneath the streetlight last night, come to save Dad's life. I just hope it's big enough.

I cut the rope that's leashing the alligator. It lunges, snaps, misses. Thrashes out. Even with an animal this size, relatively small, my leg numbs where the tail connects with a slap.

"Dad," I say. "I need you out here." I can see my father on the far side of the fence, looking in at the alligator and me, moving over the grass, the gator making short rushes and stopping and me trying to circle around it and stay out of range, grabbing at its tail.

"I need your help," I say.

"Get out of there!"

"Come help me. We'll get him somewhere safe. Take off your shirt," I say. "We'll get it on his eyes."

My father pulls off his t-shirt and walks through the metal swing gate. He joins me in the gator dance. The gator knows it too. It whips around to show its teeth. "Watch the tail," my father says. "Get behind him. You remember how to do it?"

"No," I say.

"Christ," my father says. "I'll put the shirt over his eyes. You're going to have to jump on him. Press down on his head. Press down hard and hold the mouth closed. He's not so big. He's a teenager. Are you ready?"

"No," I say. "I can't do it. I need you to do it."

"Shit, son. I'm old. Let's leave it be. Let's get in the house."

I see my father lowering the shirt, see his belly heaving with his breath. See quitting on his sweaty face. The defeat. But I am a shaman.

I take a step back and sit on the ground.

"What are you doing?"

Eye-level with the alligator, it looks bigger. The eyes are cracked yellow and black, dry grass over Lincoln River. River of my youth.

"What are you doing?"

This gator has no idea where it is now or what part it has to play in my father's salvation. It only knows itself. It only knows how to unscrew my foot from my leg after it claps on. The gator is hissing. I believe what it's saying.

"Get up!"

The gator makes its charge. Before it can snap onto my arm, my father dives onto its back. He slams the wad of his shirt over the bulges of the little alligator's eyes. He bashes and grinds his elbow into the long head. He presses and grips the jaws closed with brown, leathery hands. He's beautiful. He's divine. He's bleeding from somewhere, his nose, and crimson is smeared all across his face and dripping down his chin and over the alligator.

"Get up," he says.

I fall to my back. Feel the Earth turn. See that the tree birds are pleased by our mortal goings-on. They are flitting from limb to limb, speaking in tongues, stretching brown thrush feathers against the cold, clear sky. They are rapt in praise and witness. They are descending to join us. Winged Valkyries all around.

Tiger Drill in Butterfly Class

Preston Rigalloe is going blind. I have a slip from his mother that says so. *We trust you will deal with this gently.*

I'm watching Preston try to write a sentence involving an adjective. His face is an inch from the page. Someone could teach him braille, but in two months he'll be the middle school's problem and I'll retire to the coast. I debate ordering the books anyway, just to slide my fingertips over the bumps. Like, bump-bump. *Daiquiri.* Bump-bump. *Please.*

That's when the Big Cat Alarm starts to peal.

I have a look through the split blinds. There's a gray sky over the Play Yard, and the wind has the tall grass bent over. There are no twitching tails by the cafeteria dumpsters. Jeffers and I figure it's a drill, but we have the kids in Butterfly Class make masks just the same. And with the old zoo grounds so close, who knows what's out there, really? Not me.

Will this count toward Enrichment Hours? Jeffers asks.

Yes, yes. I wave her off and blow the Craft Whistle. The butterflies fall in behind the marker box where they're issued two primaries and an accent.

This is Jeffers' first year as a teacher's aide. She shepherds the Big Criers to the Designated Freak Out Spot as I point them out. It's just a laminated red circle taped to the floor, but the children warm to the protocol. Arms clasped across their chest, all three Jigolli sisters bend at the knees while Jeffers coaches them through respiration cycles.

Brace up, I tell the class. I model the creation of a child-sized face on a paper plate at the front of the room beneath twirling, red hazard lights. I show them how it is possible to make perfect, circular eye sockets with the bottom of a plastic cup. Do thus, I shout over the alarm, and staple yellow yarn to the paper scalp.

The alarm wails *Bee-Ohhhhhh-Bee-Ohhhhhh-Bee.*

See how I draw the eyes big and wide?

The idea is: Tigers attack where you're not looking. They don't know the plastic googly eyes aren't wired to a brain. So let's doll up those plates, says the county's Board of Education Crises. Let's get some color in those eyes. Really wow this beast.

I patrol the room, penning stray freckles and moles on the mask faces. Jeffers gives a gap-toothed girl a nasty scar. And Preston, my clever Preston, is the first to strap his paper face onto the back of his head and draw the harness string tight.

I'm moved when I see the face he's drawn. Brown irises under scribbly brown hair. A sloppy pair of eye-glasses, like bent wheels. It's me.

Is that my face? I ask.

Preston looks toward the sound of my voice. Is that my face? he parrots back. His little, chubby cheeks are pinched up around his eyes. My face? This time he says it with a lisp.

With a tiger loose, we shouldn't risk an ice cream, but I can see the ambulance-shaped creamery van idling in the pickup line.

Are you sure? Jeffers asks. She's checking her email. Looking for an All-Clear.

Let them live, I say.

Jeffers climbs to the roof with her rifle, and I slump against the brick face of the Learning Hall with the red Disaster Whistle held between my teeth. Watch the children pass with thirty masks affixed.

The Butterflies trudge arm in arm across the yard, and it is eerie—the way their faces change from human to facsimile. On one side, they're grim, focused on reaching the ice cream unmauled, keeping their zig-zagging Flee Routes clear like we've practiced, and on the other side, they're smiling, wide-eyed and vibrant in the open sun. Preston is in the middle of the chain, being led on his left and right, holding tight to his classmates with his eyes squeezed shut.

And I can see why these masks were chosen as a counter measure. How they might give a tiger pause.

Dog

Byron found the carcass of Mary's dog on the black mud of the salt marsh, behind a row of palms and within sight of the community dock. It wasn't Mary's dog really, though it had appeared regularly in her yard. It liked to dig a sleeping trench and hide inside then rush out barking when something passed by, but it always stopped short. Byron had never heard Mary call its name, so he did not know it. The dog had belonged to her mom's boyfriend, Babe, who was, himself, dead.

The body was short with square, muscled shoulders. The stomach was white with spots, each one distended now like tattoos on a pregnant belly. The fur ran from yellow to brown. Ten yards below the highwater mark, the dog lay alone on the dried and cracked mud. There were no footprints nearby, but the tide had a way of making them disappear.

The dog's eyes were open, but the lid and balls had been pecked away. Byron could see the shallow gouges where beaks had done their work. There was a hole ripped into the lower abdomen. Buzzards, gone now. Something must have scared them away, or maybe the tide had come in and covered the body. He poked at the dog with a length of palm frond. The hair was stiff with salt, and the flesh beneath did not give. The whole mass of it rocked when he pushed harder with the stick.

Byron examined the tan pads of the dog's feet, which were clean. He pulled the pads apart and felt the soft place between them like he did with his dogs at home. The smell of the body made Byron's face scrunch, but some of the old dog smell, like worn upholstery, still hung on. It might have been a good dog, he thought. Thin yellow ears hung jauntily on either side of the wide head; they were black crusted, but he could tell they had been soft. The teeth were sharp and clean.

Byron would be fourteen in a week. For his birthday, he desperately wished to increase the girth of his neck. He regretted that he hadn't asked his parents for a leather cap that he could dangle iron plates from. Instead, he had asked them for a nylon dragon kite and a Casio calculator watch. The kite he wanted for kite club, and the watch he wanted to impress his neighbor, Mary. She had not been at school today, but her mom's low-bodied, white car was in the driveway. She might be home, but Byron was afraid to knock on the door. It had been three days since he saw her, since her father had been arrested for murder.

Everyone knew the dead man. He was Mary's mother's boyfriend, Babe. Byron heard the sirens and big engines of the police on the blacktop before they arrived. They drove in a tight line, end to end, four of them, racing. The blocky Chargers rolled over the pine straw landscaping and parked like a black steel gate around Mary's dad's little black truck and Babe's red truck and the low, white car. It happened in the afternoon, about an hour after the school bus came through. Not many people were home.

Mr. Mitchel told it all at the tennis court the night after the murder, while Byron's serious father listened quietly. Byron chased stray balls or else lobbed them into the thick cobwebs that hung in the corners of the court. Mr. Mitchel's old body was buzzing with the new popularity his knowledge lent him. He was a known gossip, and it took an hour of hard tennis to learn what he knew. There had been no struggle and no chase. After it was done, Phill, who was Mary's dad, set out a folding chair in the garage and waited for the police to arrive, while Jill ran to the Mitchels' house to make the call.

"Where was Mary?" Byron asked.

"I don't know, son." Mr. Mitchel said. "She came in and sat with Mrs. Jill soon enough."

He told them that Mrs. Mitchel had run a cool bath for Mary. Then Jill used the phone to call her mother, while at Jill's house, Phill sat in the garage and smoked. When the deputies arrived, he walked out with his hands up. "I saw them pull the cigarette out of his mouth," Mr. Mitchel said. "Like a movie."

"What kind of gun was it?" Byron's father asked while bouncing a tennis ball on his racket.

Mr. Mitchel shook his head. "I asked Jill—she couldn't tell me. I asked the sheriff—he *wouldn't* tell me. I'm thinking it was that Colt clone he carried around 'fer snakes.' Some real Dirty Harry shit. Twelve years, he lived here."

"That's a .44," Byron said, but he kept his eyes on the folds of the cobwebs on his tennis ball, hoping the men would forget. What did it matter?

"What you say?" His father was frowning at him.

"Dirty Harry used a .44."

"You might have a little killer in you yet, boy." Mr. Mitchel smiled. ".44 would have taken his head off."

Whatever Babe's real name was, no one had used it. For the last year, his red truck had been seen outside of Jill's house—sometimes for days at a time. At the neighborhood oyster roast, everyone pretended to know what he did for work. Some agreed that he built dog boxes and shipped them across the country. Another heard he welded submarines at King's Bay.

"A scuba welder," Mrs. Stanley confirmed with a nod. "Very skilled. I've seen the gas tanks."

Since he separated from Jill, Phill's truck was a rarity. He came some weekends to take Mary to dinner or maybe a movie, but Mary talked to Byron like the divorce was certain. All but done.

"He was a real nice boy, Babe," Mr. Mitchel told Byron's father. "Filled our tires with his compressor. He helped me put up my Christmas lights this year. On a ladder."

Last summer, Babe took Jill out on a double-seater kayak. Byron and Mary had watched the adults from the community dock as they wove through the marsh to a woody island.

"They're fucking," Mary said. It was the first time they had talked about anything like that. They'd come to swim, and Mary was in her suit. She leaned against the dock's concrete piling and scratched at bugs in her hair. Thin blue veins shown through the skin of her hips. Byron glanced at the silver stubs glinting over her bikini.

"Maybe," he said.

"They're not married."

Byron laughed. "Mary and Joseph weren't married."

"Jill doesn't even tan. Now she's fucking in the marsh."

Byron wondered who Mary knew that was having sex. He thought of Jonathan Hitchens, who was fully six feet by eighth grade. He had grandparents here and visited most summers.

Mary cut her eyes. "It's disgusting. You meet someone for one year, you don't know where they were the last one. Where does he go when he's not here?"

"He's from Savannah."

"What do you know about it? You don't know about sex."

Why was she barbing him? He brushed it off. It excited him to see the flipped kayak on the shore of the island. He liked to think of what Jill and Babe were doing out there. "I know what sex is."

Mary winced like she'd been stuck between the eyes.

"What?" Byron asked.

"It's dong brain, dude. She can't think straight."

Byron stayed for dinner at Mary's that night. Jill and Babe boiled pasta and drizzled oil over thick toast. They ridiculed the radio's local ads and sang along with the hits while the sauce warmed. Everyone but Mary. *I like it. I love it. I want some more of it.* Mary faked a gag. Still, to Byron it felt nice. Only once, at a funeral, had he seen his parents holding hands. Jill and Babe were always touching. Byron spent the dinner with his left hand on his knee beneath the table, brushing the thin hairs that grew out of his skin and wishing

Mary would put her hand under the table too.

"Why do you hate him so much?" Byron asked her before he went home for the night. They were in the dark of Mary's garage, batting the tennis ball that hung from the ceiling back and forth.

"He's just getting settled now," Mary said. "That's why he plays it so shweet."

"I think you're sweet," Byron said.

"Yeah? You want to fuck me, Baby Byron?" She called him that sometimes, even though they were the same age.

"I guess," he said, even though he had never said the word "fuck" before. Even "shit" or "ass" was enough to get his tongue covered in liquid dish soap at home.

"Well, keep guessing," Mary said. They never spoke of it again.

***

Mary was not at school the day after the murder, or yesterday, or today. Byron was not surprised by her absence. He was only curious. On the mudflat, he noticed that the dead dog's toenails were neatly trimmed. It was a house dog. He didn't think Mary would miss it.

"Sorry about Babe," Byron said to the dog, practicing for when he saw Mary. It sounded empty. He tried again. "You've been gone, and I missed you." An ant crawled out of the dead dog's eye hole, walked the length of its snout, and entered a nostril. Byron lifted the dog's head and peered into its nose, but the ant was already gone.

"Baby Byron?" Mary's voice called from the palm brush-forest. A second later, she broke through the wood line and began walking toward Byron and the dog. Her long, fine hair was twisted into a thick, white rope that hung off the back of her head.

"Don't call me that," Byron said. He noticed that her Casio watch was gone.

When Mary was near enough, she pinched the short hairs on the back of Byron's neck with her fingers and gave two short tugs down. It had been a bully fad of their elementary school days. Byron jerked his arm to peel her hand away, but it was already gone. "The shit?" he said.

"Who's your friend?" Mary asked. She was chewing her gum too hard, and she sounded funny. She was touching him and joking around like she never did. Years later, he would feel foolish for not knowing she was drunk.

"This?" Byron pointed to the dog.

"Yes 'this.' I'm fucking with you. I know who this is." But she hadn't looked at the dog yet. She only nodded toward it.

Byron hadn't expected Mary to cry over the dog, but he had expected something. "Oh," he said. "I'm sorry. I heard about it all," he said.

"You heard about it *all*?" Mary made her face go slack and let her arms hang at her sides. It was her "dumbass" face. She walked to a lumpy azalea bush and stared into its branches.

"Most of it. Is your mom okay?"

"Well, if you know it all, you know she's fine. Mitchel told you?"

Byron threw his palm frond sword into the mud flat; the blade sang whiffle notes when it twisted in the air. "You've been gone," he said.

"I'm glad he's dead," Mary said. "Babe."

"Why?"

"You know how gross he was. Always kissing on Mom. Feeling her legs when I was around."

"I guess."

"Dad shot him here," Mary pointed to a place an inch above her right eye. She had a flat red freckle on the spot. "The bullet went through and into the wall. The cops pulled it out." She smiled. Her thin teeth looked like chips of ice. Something blue had collected in grooves in the enamel and on the serrations on their flat, razor edges. "Did Mitchel know that?"

Bryon drew a line in the mud with the toe of his sneaker, circling the dog, but imagining what Mr. Mitchel had said. That the Dirty

Harry gun would have taken Babe's head off. His knees felt loose and strange beneath him. He wished he had not thrown his stick.

"He kept trying to get her on his side. He kept trying to be all sweet, and Mom bought it. It was so annoying," Mary said while she dug in the leaves inside the azalea. Then she pulled out a gun.

It was a small, black revolver with a wooden handle. The kind a detective might carry, or an old city cop. Byron's grandfather had been a police officer in Detroit. He and his father drove to the county range once to shoot his old service pistol before it was sealed under a frame. It was almost the same.

"Where did you get that?"

"It was Babe's," she said. "He doesn't need it now. And it doesn't belong in my house."

"Why do you have it?"

Mary walked back to the dog with the gun. "Look. Babe was trying to get sweet and brought this dog to our house. Adopted it. Made Mom name it. But nobody asked for that," she said.

"Oh." Byron's hands were sweating and sticking together. He rubbed them on his jeans. He had seen handguns before, their handles stuck out of jeans or laid in the bottom of purses. This was, he realized, the first gun he had ever been afraid of. He didn't know why Mary had hidden it out here or what she wanted to do.

"And then the dog is some maniac who barks like he's going to tear your face off. Nobody asked for *that*. And then Dad shows up and starts telling Babe how he's ruining our family, and you know what happened then."

"Yeah."

"Yeah, well I went and got this gun because I didn't know what was going to happen. I didn't want to get shot. Not by Babe." She said his name like it was a joke.

"Fuck," Byron said, but Mary didn't notice. She was talking to herself and sucking in air. She was sweating. Her face seemed to glow.

"So I get down the stairs with the gun and everyone's gone

except the dead guy and I didn't know what to do with the gun so I came here to throw it in the water, and that's when this thing," she pointed the gun at the dog, "comes after me. Tries to bite me. Well, that was that." Mary's blue eyes shrank into red slits that bled tears.

"You shot it?"

"I tried to scare it off, but things got fucky."

"Why?"

"Why what? What would you have done?"

"It didn't do anything. Why do you have the gun?" He knew he was crying, and he closed his back teeth onto his tongue.

"It doesn't matter if you like it or not." She looked at the dog. She seemed afraid it would stand up. Then she took a couple of crow hops on the mud flat, like she was going to throw the gun, but stopped.

"We should bury it. The mud will eat it up."

"Take it to the police."

"Don't cry, baby," she said. She touched Byron's cheek with the tip of her finger. "These things happen. And soon, other things will happen. No one will be thinking about Babe in a year. No one cared about his dog. They were intruders. Like an invasive species." She sounded like she was saying lines. "They didn't belong." Mary gagged and a long line of spit hung out of her mouth. "Gross," she said, and pulled the thread from her lips to flick on the ground.

Byron's head felt light. A week ago, he had walked with Mary here. They collected brown and green bits of glass. They found some kind of long, bony ray that had beached itself and lay dying in an inch of water. The gills had maggots in them. When Byron jammed a stick through the ray's head, the tail slashed the air. He imagined that day and today rubbing against each other through invisible walls, and he pretended he could slide back in time. If it weren't for the dog and the gun, he would be there.

"Do you want to shoot it? There's still bullets." Mary held the gun out to Byron.

"What? No, I don't want to."

"If you don't, it's because you'll tell," she said.

"I won't tell."

"You might."

"I won't."

"Have you ever shot anything before?" She aimed the gun at Byron's foot, and watched him step back.

"Stop that."

She smiled with her blue teeth, and pulled the hammer of the revolver back with her whole left hand until it clicked and clicked again.

"Someone will hear."

"Shoot the dog."

"I don't want to."

"You can kiss me."

Byron could barely hear her. There seemed to be a high wail emitting from the cocked gun. It sounded like the drug officer's crime videos at school and his mother's chide and a political ad with big red Xs all mixed together and shouting for him to freeze, to run, to do something loud. This was important, he thought. Why couldn't he move? This was one of those important times. "That's okay," he said

"You don't want to?" Mary dug in her pocket. "You want someone else now?"

"No." Byron watched the gun in her other hand. The barrel swung all over. This new Mary stood close to him. He didn't recognize the way she hovered around the dog and needed to hurt it, to tear it up. In the summers, she and Byron saved turtles from swimming pools. They followed birds tree to tree. For an entire day, they trailed a cat that came off a boat in the marina, trying to feed it. To pet it. Then they found a thin green snake trapped in the side mirror of a car and stripped its skin off trying to pull it loose. It looked like electrical wires. Mary had never asked Byron to kiss her before.

Mary's hand came out of her pocket with a piece of gum. She popped it into her mouth.

"One kiss. One shot." She held out the gun to Byron again, the barrel pointing at his stomach.

Byron stepped close to her and took the gun. He aimed it at the dog and the dark hole Mary had already shot into it. Just one, he thought. It can't feel anything. Then I can go home.

"First," Mary said, and reached her arm around Byron's waist. She grabbed at his skinny buttocks and pulled him until his hips touched her own. Their foreheads bumped gently. Mary matched her lips to Byron's, and he felt the hard muscle of her tongue slide between his teeth and knock around the inside of his mouth. Her spit tasted sweet. Her eyes looked into his. They were raw from crying. It was his first kiss, and it carried a current that made his limbs seem to separate at their joints. Even with the dog and the teeth and the gun, it was good. Mary could see what he was feeling. How could he hide? She held him by the chin and pulled her face away.

"I knew I could trust you."

"Why are you doing this?" Byron asked.

"You're the only one who can know what happened." They were still close to one another, and, for a moment, Mary hung around his neck. She spoke into his scalp, as if directly to his brain. "We can control what happens to us. You know what I know. Together." Then she took hold of his hand, which still held the cocked pistol, and raised it to the dog.

Byron's hands felt far away, and he wondered if there was a rock buried in the mud that might send the shot into his own face instead of the dog's. It was dead, he thought. He closed his eyes. He squeezed the trigger slowly until the hammer dropped and the gun kicked in his hand. The report drove a black bird from an oak. An egret glared from across the marsh. That was all.

"You missed," Mary said.

Byron opened his eyes. There was a clean, circular gouge in the mud just below the dog's head. It might have been a fiddler crab hole—one of millions. Relief and nausea rolled in him, and his shoulders sagged against Mary. She held him upright. She pulled him close with her fingers hooked through the belt loops of his jeans.

"Yeah." He tried to pull away, but Mary held on.

"One more," she said. "It doesn't work if you don't do it."

"I don't want to. What doesn't work?"

"We won't be the same," she said softly, still holding on to his pants and pulling him now, just a little to the side, so that he had to step with her toward the dog. Like a dance.

"Mary."

She kissed him again, sucking at his lower lip. It was spearmint on her spit. It was rock candy with some kind of bite. What was it? When their lips parted, Byron leaned against her and breathed the melon-scented shampoo she wore. She squeezed her arms around his back, and her strength surprised him. He began to wonder if they would keep meeting like this. The smell of the carcass rose between them.

"Shoot it this time. With your eyes open," Mary said. She reached for the pistol in his hand. She cocked it roughly and wrapped her hand around his and the wooden grip of the gun.

"Wait," he said.

"How do you feel?" she asked. She bent at the knees, pulling Byron by the hand until he too was crouched over the dog, and then she pressed the pistol against its bloated side. The smell of rot laced with the melon—sugar-sick.

"God, it stinks."

Mary leaned in to kiss him once more. She moved her finger inside the trigger guard and laid it over his own. "You're fine," she breathed.

"No," Byron said, and shoved her away. He shot the gun in the air, ducking like an idiot and afraid. He worked the pistol's action and fired two more times into the mud then dropped the gun. While Mary fumed, he stared at the perfect indentation of the pistol on the cracked mud, which itself looked as rich and sweet as brownie batter. Then his stomach pumped out the chocolate powder shake he'd drank after school.

"You didn't have to waste all the shots," Mary said.

"Shut up."

She watched him closely.

Byron looked back at the dog and imagined Mary leading it out, her spindly hand wrapped beneath its collar to the hard mud. "You did a bad thing," he said.

Mary rolled her eyes. "OK, Byron. You stuff toads with leaves."

He had stuffed toads with leaves. A neighbor's nephew had caught them and held their mouths open while Byron thumb-pushed clumps of crackling orange leaves deep inside, like a pocket. He was too young to remember how many times they did this. They were never caught. He had told Mary all of this the night of the pasta and Tim McGraw. She had asked him to tell her a secret.

Byron put his hand on Mary's arm, but she pushed it off. "I won't tell," he said. "But we'll both know. Like the toads."

"You're going to grow up to be a serial killer," she said. "You're going to stuff people like that."

"I hope not." He stooped and dug his arms under the carcass until he had the dog secure against his body. The dry fur rested beneath his chin. The dog was heavy. Something cold ran across his hand.

"What are you doing?" Mary asked.

"Take the gun."

Mary picked up the gun and followed Byron across the marsh to the community dock. She threw the pistol into the water.

No one else was on the river. Palms leaned over the water from the mud bank behind them, as if straining to get a closer look, their root-ball feet clinging to the shore. Dead trees lay snaking and gray under the surface, all of them reached toward the dock where Mary and Byron stood. A hard wind blew off the sound and tore a few dead fronds from the palm trees, carrying them like dandelion spores.

Byron held the dog over the water. "Do you want to say anything about it?"

"What? Jesus, throw it in."

"This is the last time we'll see it," he said. He hoped it wouldn't float back to shore, but it might. An image of him and Mary stuffing the dog's mouth and throat with busted pieces of concrete forced itself on him. "I wish I had said something about the toads."

Mary was silent. "You think I'm evil?"

"We did a bad thing," he said. He didn't know what they could do about it now, but he wanted to do something.

"So what? It's done."

A man shouted from somewhere on the land above the dock. Someone coming to investigate the shots.

"We've got to go," Mary said. She grasped at his sleeve, but he still held the dog. She didn't want to get too close.

"What was its name?" he asked.

"It was a creep's dog. Byron, c'mon."

"It's not his dog anymore," Byron said. He turned the eyeless yellow lump toward her. "It's just a dead dog. Give it something." His arms were burning and beginning to straighten so that he had to use the tops of his thighs to hold the body. "Hurry."

"It was Ox," she said. "Goodbye, Ox." She curtsied.

Byron let the dog fall into the river. From behind him, he heard the ringing of Mary's shoes on the steel ramp of the community dock. Then she was talking to whoever was up there. Telling them, no, she didn't know. No, she didn't hear the gun.

The carcass hung just beneath the surface of the dark green water. Byron pushed it with his hand, but it bobbed back up. He knew he was connected to Mary in a new way now, but he was sure she wasn't right, after all, when she said they could control what happened to them. How could they when things kept happening? One thing after the next. Piling up. Washing in from secret, gruesome places.

ELSOHN

In a barn marked "Sit-A-While," a man in a black rain slicker stands where I left the Elsohn boy. He's an old, calcified sort. I'm thinking, "Take him, Pappy. Please." He picks the boy up from the table of blankets—turning him like an apple in the light. He wipes the baby's mouth with the side of his thumb and rocks him, murmuring and looking around the room until he sees me watching.

"Is this your boy?" he asks. His eyes run me over, memorizing my face and hair. Approximate height and weight. His hair is buzzed short, sharp and gray.

"No," I say.

"Was someone here?"

"No."

"Are you sure?" He crosses the barn floor with the boy.

I am digging and turning my hands in a plastic bin of mated socks, reaching deeper and feeling out the corners for the pair that will convince the old man to walk the other way.

"Hold him," the old man says, and presses the Elsohn boy against my arm. He is already releasing his hold before I can speak. From his back pocket, the old man produces a push-to-talk radio that I hadn't noticed before, the sort with a long antenna that can call out to space.

He starts to chatter, "Waters, Malthus. Waters, Malthus." He coughs and spits. A response comes, and the old man, Waters, shoots back and forth with whoever is on the other end, telling them all about the boy he found, while the boy himself sleeps on my chest, wetting my shirt and stretching his legs.

This morning, I drove five hours to take the Elsohn boy to the Malthus stores across the state and leave him. It's Sunday, the day the country people come to shop and pass talk. The Malthus stores are all built in the shells of old barns. They stand in a line and look out over fallow fields, now roped off for a parking lot. The silos are covered in climbing vines. It is fall, and behind the barns, the Berkshires have the shape of a woman under a mottled quilt, their peaks soft as hips and rolling down to nothing.

I left the boy in the barn where they sell rocking chairs and those rough blankets patterned in Southwestern motifs. I set him on a stack of those blankets like he was a shirt or something that I'd picked up in the store, carried for a time, and put down. Except, of course, this is different. This is a child, just a few months old.

Even after leaving him, I couldn't help but watch the way he slept. Like a man moving in waist-high water, Elsohn is wading through whatever dreams come to an infant boy, pushing through them with his eyes squeezed shut and his mouth twisting up and smoothing out in the wake of what's flickering behind those tissue-paper lids. Probably just shapes and smells and half-things: half-trucks and half-green flies and half-cooked notions of hands and blankets and me.

He appeared at dawn in the front seat of my truck. Wispy insect nymphs circled his face. His mother—if she is his mother—was a girl I never knew. I looked for her face in the Elsohn boy's but couldn't remember what to look for. If she had his blue eyes or drooping cheeks or his crimped, elfish ears. I had met her in a circle of trucks and fucked her in the bed of one of them. It was late, and the bonfire was dead. She wore a leather jacket that reached her knees and fanned out beneath her like a heavy sheet. But was it brown or was it black? Had she spoken with a Boston hitch? I never asked.

Sari called the child Elsohn for the road I live on. Elsohn Drive. It's better, I think, that we don't give him a proper name. "Busy morning for you," she said, peeking into the folds of his blanket. "Is it yours?"

"No way to know."

"There's ways," she said. She was dressed for work, her white coat and antique medicine bag. She showed pity and wiped his ass with her rubber gloves on. She felt his head. She told me to call the sheriff. Then she gathered herself into a misty cloud and disappeared on the wind, or she would, I knew. It was to be freedom. The high, crisping desert. She is deep in arrangements. Faraway, a team of realtors, headhunters, and sister-doctor-friends all search at her command. I had decided months ago to follow Sari to Tucson or Taos or whatever place she wants to go. I told her: just spin a wheel.

Anyone who knows me here knows I blew things with the Navy, sold family land, and showed my ass to true love. My mother and her brothers are gone, but the shop owners keep them alive when they whisper to their teenaged clerks: "That's the one what ran the dairy into the ground." Hallelujah: Sari knows who I am and doesn't seem to care. I think she likes it, even. I won't slow her down. "You don't look like a farmer to me," she says.

"I'm not."

In the barn, Waters is making his report into the radio, and the Elsohn boy is crying in my arms. I'm shushing and rocking and trying to ignore the particular angle that his brow meets his nose. In my pocket are two rings of turquoise, found in one of the neighboring barns.

We'll have a wedding on the dunes, Sari and me. And a cake the shape of a cactus rose. I'll show her what good I can do. Desert-good that I don't even know about yet. Say, making a flat-bottom sailboat to move over the sand. The lizards will come skittering from beneath their rocks when we pass, drawn by the glare of sun on tin.

Waters locks eyes on me. "What are you? MacTaggart? Sheehan?"

"No," I say.

"Stay here," he says, and walks out.

And there I am again with the Elsohn boy in the Sit-A-While, and I have a choice. The same choice I had an hour ago, but now it's different with Waters and his radio. If I leave, there will be questions. Someone might know me, even here. Witnesses could appear. There was the smoking woman who cooed at the Elsohn boy while I walked between the barns, deciding where he would go. Would she remember my face?

I leave the barn with the Elsohn boy tucked into my arm. His body swells with every breath. I think of pink-skinned poultry chicks, how their hearts rage visibly beneath the skin.

My truck is parked in the shadow of a willow stand. I should have parked farther out. Through my windshield, I look for Waters and see black clouds instead. The skies darken. The willows stir. There is the quick, sullen drama of a valley storm, boring like a rerun. In May, the rain comes every day.

The Sit-A-While is a rotten jack-o-lantern in its field with a barn door mouth and hayloft window eyes. A worker closes one of the windows with a long, metal pole, then the other. The face of the barn is passive; it does not care if I leave the child or not. It does not care about anything or even remember when it housed horses or hoppers or whatever it was that they did on this farm. The barn doesn't care, and the willow doesn't care, and the mountains don't care either. The smoking woman agrees: the Elsohn boy could be anywhere or with anyone, but he doesn't have to be here or with Sari and me. I feel tremendous power in deciding where to plant him. Not here, I decide. I had lingered too long, dithering. Too many people had seen my face.

The roads around Malthus are winding with thin shoulders and narrow, grassy dips that stand for a ditch. We pass through one valley and into another. Night arrives. I keep the radio low. The Elsohn boy is asleep in the crease of my passenger seat, and his hands are clinching and reaching to cover his eyes. Somewhere in the back of my mind, I am reminded that he may scratch himself. I reach over to feel if his finger nails are sharp like a puppy's teeth, but they're soft and wet.

The body of a deer appears, white in the headlights. I lift my foot from the pedal too late, and the deer is crushed. The cab rushes in, and when I wake the radiator is hissing vitriol, busted to hell with the front of the truck. The truck's blinker is click-clinking, locked in a forever left.

The animal is on the hood. A doe. One of her legs is sticking through the windshield, drooping dead. I think of the deer's hoof slashing around the inside of the truck's cab while I was slack in the seat, and my throat gets tight. I unclench my jaw. I taste the grit between my teeth.

I see the passenger seat empty and I remember, all at once, the boy. I sit upright. On the floorboard, the baby coughs. The boot heater is rasping on his head. Blue-tinted duty-glass dusts his wrap. I watch my hands reach out and pick the shards away and lift him from the floor. Globs of red bloom across his forehead, and my breath catches before I realize it is my own blood and wipe it from the child's face with the tail of my shirt.

I set the Elsohn boy back in his seat and cut the engine. Outside, the front left tire is bent in, and I know the truck is done. In a fog, I wrap a dirty shirt around my head. The smell of chemical steam hangs around. I see the reaching, yellow light of a house and the familiar shapes of barn and silo hulking nearby.

It will take some time to reach the house, but there will be a phone. I'm not sure who I will call. No wrecker. No police. Not Sari, who will be coming back from Millerton about now and expecting me at home, ready to tell her how I worked it all out. But I need a ride. There's no one else to call.

Walking with the Elsohn boy, I pass a concrete mailbox made into the shape of a dolphin. Oyster and conch shells lie in a heap around its base. In the frontage field, many half-dead apple trees persist. Their trunks are twisted and parched. As I walk between the rows, I wonder what fills the farmer's silo or if it's just for show.

The screen door on the house whines open, and a woman steps out. As I get closer, she raises her hand. "Was that you what crashed?" She does not seem very old, though her hair is silver. "Is that a baby?"

"It is. Can I use your phone?"

"Of course," she says. "I just called the sheriff."

I feel the air close over my head like a ziplock bag and, instinctually, turn toward the truck. I can just see the outline of it. The reflective strips catching the lights of a passing car. The line of the road runs along the bottom of the valley for miles. There's nowhere to go but forward and back. I sit down at the dolphin woman's kitchen table. The wallpaper is all pastel shells over pale white sand.

The dolphin woman points me to a blue phone hanging on the wall and gestures for the child. "Can I see him? Are you sure he's fine?"

I pass the Elsohn boy to her and dial Sari's mobile phone number—she is the only person I know with a mobile phone. The dolphin woman checks around the boy's head. She looks into his eyes. She holds him up beneath the light in the kitchen and smiles when he makes some startled, garbled sound. I should know her, I think. My house is ten miles away. I should at least know *of* her. I wonder what she knows about me.

Sari answers the phone. "Yes?" she says through static.

"I hit a deer. Can you pick me up? I'm down County 7 from the fairgrounds. Toward home."

"God knows," she says. "Do you still have the Elsohn boy?"

The dolphin woman lays the child on the kitchen table, and points to my brow, where I've bound the cut. "Can I see that?" she whispers. "I was a nurse."

I nod and feel the cool rush of blood as she unties the shirt. She pulls a medical kit from above a cabinet and begins to clean the wound.

"I have him," I say into the phone. "Come pick me up, and we'll talk about it." The line pops and fizzles. "Sari?"

"Did you talk to the cops?" Sari asks.

"I'll work it out. Just look for my truck on the road."

"You'll tell them it's not your kid?"

"Yeah. We'll talk when you're here."

"Okay," Sari says, and hangs up. She always does that, always ends the conversation without "goodbye." She says it is a boring tradition. The little dance people do at the end of a phone call.

I sit back down in my chair. I consider that she may leave me in this valley, and it makes my scalp itch.

"How long have you lived here?" I ask the dolphin woman, and wonder how long it will be before Waters arrives and asks me, again, if the boy is my son. And if I say he isn't, what then?

"A year," the dolphin woman says, and pours a cup of coffee. "My husband and I moved from Mississippi last summer." She raises a spoon to me and I nod. I try to remember who owned this land ten years ago. I think of how far away the back wall of the valley is—too far to run. I think of my one-time-pastor uncle who lived in secret and worked a mountain still through the night. He was never caught by a badge. When the congregation found out what he was doing, they marched on his cabin in the woods and dragged him out of it. Somebody here always knows where you are.

The dolphin woman passes me a hot mug. *All weather*, it reads in letters made of umbrellas and shells, *is beach weather.*

I wonder if she might take the boy. Could I just hand him over? Just like that?

"You two are lucky," she says. "I could hear that crash from here." She shakes the Elsohn boy's hand, and the hoop bracelets she wears jangle. The boy is lying in the middle of the dolphin woman's kitchen table—exactly where the turkey would go, or the ham.

"Do you have something we could put him in?" I ask. "Anything will do." Beneath his towel wrap, he is wearing the same black t-shirt that I put him in this morning. It fits him like a judge's gown. My

57

blood shines on the sleeve. A rash has bloomed on his cheek.

As soon as the dolphin woman leaves the room, I snatch up the phone and dial Sari again.

"Come get me," I say when I hear her breathing on the line. "Come get me and let's get out of here. Go to the desert." She is quiet for a while. I say, "Hurry up."

It's not right, she says, to put this on her. She has her practice. She has her plans.

"*We've* got plans. I love you," I say, but it comes out halting and embarrassed and not like love at all.

She says, "I dunno, Casey," and kills the call.

The dolphin woman comes back a little later with a pair of faded blue boxers and a small fleece blanket. I step out on the porch to smoke while she fastens the clothes together with safety pins. Outside, I feel the absence of the boy. Something like when you walk away from your wallet or some other thing you've joined to yourself, fixed in your mind.

"Do you have people to come get you?" the dolphin woman asks from the doorway. She has the boy in her arms and she looks, I can say with certainty, beautiful in the soft light of her beach-themed home.

"Not really."

"You new here?"

I shake my head.

"I can take you once the rain is past."

The air outside is cold and witchy, pressed against the valley's floor and squeezing between its ridges. I dream a future: Elsohn and me in the old whiskey camp. The boy learns to totter around the stove, while I stack cairn stones to mark the years. I try to run away, but a posse of shave-head sheriffs guard the mountain passes. Then the whole valley shows up with the tar-and-feather bath. I dream another where the boy grows up on the family farm. He comes of age and leaves with Sari Segal for the desert, but I am an old man. I stack ancient, frozen cow pies to mark the years.

"Won't you hold him?" the dolphin woman asks.

I smash my cigarette into the half clamshell that she has on her little porch. There are already twenty or so butts in it. I reach out for the still, potato-bodied boy. He smells like a blown airbag.

The close-set headlights of Sari's jeep emerge on the highway and begin to crawl toward us. From the other direction, the blue lights of the sheriff appear. The two cars barrel down on each other like knights in a joust, except Sari drives past the dolphin mailbox, and the sheriff stops at the wreck.

I imagine laying the boy down in a rocking chair and sprinting for Sari over the mounds of field mud and tripping apple roots. I make believe she slows the jeep to a stop and pops open the door. I see us speed away, down and out of the valley, and it's as real to me as a cactus rose whose season I never knew. If it's a green and hairy bloom or red as lips. Finally, the storm opens up. The rain combs the orchard and blows a mist onto the porch.

"Is he your son?" the dolphin woman asks.

"I don't know."

The boy's eyelashes look fully formed to me. Following someone's blueprint, I don't know. They hang in the air, dark and adult, but the rest of him has a long way to go.

"I'm Karla," the dolphin woman says. I can barely hear her. There is, all around, the grating chime of the rain on the corrugated roof.

I sit down in one of Karla's wicker rockers with the boy in my lap, and she settles into another. We can see the sheriff's big flashlight working over the truck. "I'm Casey," I say. "This is Elsohn."

Godbomb

There's a bomb in the water. Off the coast of Tybee Island, Georgia, where the wind skims salt off the Atlantic to coat your hair. The beach ends in a lump of trampled sugar dunes, and the dunes end in weeds and a split rail fence, and around the fence are Mountain Dew bottles and cigarette butts and a man sleeping in someone's abandoned towel, and beyond that the locals and retirees mingle and bump in cinderblock bars painted yellow and blue. And the people in the bars might talk about the bomb too. It's not a secret that it exists.

The blast radius is something like a mile. That's enough to eat the beach strip. Third degree burns will be doled out until the ten-mile mark—that's enough to give the fat-cat marsh mansions on Wilmington Island a tan. I can imagine it, the detonation so long after the bomb went under the waves in the fifties. The water rising up asudden, atomic steam tearing into town and flattening the little bars, the snow cone joint, the bumper pool place. God knows what'll set it off after all these years. An underwater rift will open and the Earth will clamp it in the fissure, squeeze it to bursting. Maybe the core has been decaying this whole time—collecting heat in some arcane conversion and that'll be the trigger for a chain of deathly math, some equation that takes sixty years to reach its sum, and the bomb has been waiting smugly in the black water and gray-sand bottom, dreaming of mushroom cloud sheep while the white bottoms of snowbird feet go flashing overhead and aluminum beer cans settle like fresh powder on the ocean floor.

There are a good many cans around the bomb. I'll collect them and marvel how they reappear the next week, rolling on their side so far down in the water, slowly rocking back and forth with the tide, as if on the moon. See them winking in the bent light. An invitation. I have a mesh bag that I take along, and that, besides my snorkel and fins, is all I take when I slip the boat from the dock on Saturday mornings and beat it against the tide. I dive around and look for trash, fish, whatever, always working my way to the little Styrofoam float I have roped to the bottom near the bomb. The float is, and might be, any piece of trash, if you didn't know better. Over the island, the heads of the lighthouse and the city watertank look out at the sea, and the bomb waits.

Do you believe in God? And if so, can you slip your hand beneath his shirt? Feel his chest rising? Or is that not allowed?

This isn't idol worship, what I do, but if you fill your lungs with air and dive down, letting the anchor line lead you until it turns to chain and then a gray-steel foot, and if you pick the trash from around your god's drowned body and, as you do, feel his heat emanating, real or imagined, what would you do next? Would you have the courage to keep it to yourself? Would you have the courage to come up for air and return? To press your body against the vessel and search for where the chemical warmth feels most real in your hand? Slide your fingers beneath the fins and fans and guidance equipment. Feel it, not angry or omniscient but alive. Feel it, the summit of creation—the single cell that split to grow a tail and a brain and then a high altitude bomber and this shell, like a cell, for an atom to split and scatter you to the stars. From whence you came and may come again— maybe you have, countless times, come again. Anyway, I have that kind of courage.

I'm not crazy. I don't want the bomb to blow. But, when I dig my feet into the sand and lift my mask so far down in the murk. When

I press my bare face to the rusty steel and listen for whatever kind of heartbeat lives inside. I imagine it still—the blast.

When I get home, wet suit zipped down to my navel and tied around my waist, I empty my mesh bag in the garage sink and sort the haul. Twelve beer or soda cans, I recycle. Four knots of fishing line and a pile of plastic shreds, I toss. One large conch shell, I soak in a bleach-water mix. I rent a little townhouse from the pastor, who is also my boss. There are leftovers in the refrigerator, and the day is mine, to read on the couch or turn on the TV and fall asleep to what comes on, with the door open and the noises of town drifting in. I have a good thing, and I know it.

Beside the sink, the garage phone is chiming in its dock. The caller-ID numbers parade across its little screen. It's Degan. When I answer, he hangs up. I call back and he does it again. I call back again, and he lets it ring three times before he picks up the receiver, holds it in the air so that I can hear the news or the AM/FM radio or whatever he's got going. Then he smashes it back down.

This is the shit that pisses me off. This game. Degan is a coworker and a friend. Every Monday, the pastor drops off a black bin of tracts, tri-folded parables, and invitations to be saved, and Degan and I, we pass them out. Right now, Degan is sitting in his apartment, on the hard pleather couch that rides like a park bench. He's got the phone laid out on the coffee table and his cigarettes next to it and maybe that gummed-up shit-knife he carries next to that. He's waiting on me to get in my car, or else—he'd love this— run across Tybee Island to beat on his door and demand he open up so I can talk him down from running that rusted, dull folder over his arms and legs. Then he'll go off on a rant about religion or Brazil or cry a little and close the folder knife, and we'll watch whatever has been on TV this whole time. A Lifetime special. A children's show, passing Evan Williams back and forth and listening to Mr. Rogers croon.

Those are the rules. That's what Degan expects. Expects because, three times this month, I've played along. I wish he'd just ask me to come watch TV. This time, I don't go upstairs for my keys. I call the pastor.

"This is very serious," he says.

"Yes," I say.

"Do you want me to call the police?"

"No. I don't think that would be good."

"Right, right."

"I was hoping you might talk to him," I say. "With scripture." Degan is born-again. I am when it suits me.

"Right." The pastor is a young man, a well-heeled second son from Savannah proper, from the road you see on all the postcards with the oaks reaching over the street and mingling like lover-tongues and hanging moss for the painters to paint. Maybe he hasn't done this sort of thing before. "I'll come pick you up," he says.

"Just meet me there," I say. "He's bad off."

"Right."

I hose the salt out of my hair in the garage and change into dry clothes. When I get to Degan's place, another townhouse owned by the pastor or the pastor's family or however it works, the pastor is staring into Degan's open trashcan and fishing around in it with a stick.

"Kittens," he says. "Three kittens." He's wearing his blue suit and a tie with little Golgothan hills and crosses running down to his belt.

I fish the kittens out and close the lid. They're white, and the fleas show plain through the fur. The pastor picks one up and holds it to his suit, where the thing sticks its claws into the lapel. "Maybe it'll calm him," the pastor says.

"Maybe. Let's go." I knock on the door.

"What?" Degan yells from inside.

"Saw you called," I say. "You mind if I come in?"

I can hear him walking to the door. The wood gives a little heave when he leans against it. "It's like last time," Degan says.

"I'm sorry about that. I've got the pastor here. He wanted to come see you."

"And a little guy we found downstairs!" the pastor calls. The kitten is stabbing his way to the pastor's shoulder. I imagine the fleas feeling the pastor's warmth and launching their boarding parties. Leaping through the air. For them, it will feel a hundred yards.

"What?"

"Just open up and we'll talk about it," I say. "It'll be ok, D."

The door swings open, and Degan is already walking back to his couch. "Look," he says. "I know I've been having a hard time lately, and I appreciate you coming."

The pastor, the kitten, and I shuffle in and close the door. Inside, it's cold. Degan has the window unit screaming.

I check the fridge for beer. In the cabinet over the refrigerator, I know, is a loaded revolver. I could pocket it now, but then Degan'd just use a knife if he really wanted to end it. And then he'd likely botch it. I could take every sharp thing in the house and staple bubble wrap to the walls, and he could zip tie blocks to his feet and jump off the dock. When someone wants to do the thing, there's not much you can do about it, I think. All he has to do is stop taking in air, if that's what he wants. But I don't think it is. I leave the gun. When my father took his life, he drank himself stupid and ran his truck into a dumpster. But if I had to guess, it was his own expectations that killed him. He drew the mark to meet above his head. Every day, he drew it again.

"Everyone struggles," the pastor says, and sits down on the couch next to Degan. I can feel him warming up. The services I've attended; he always starts like this. A little universality. "This kitten, even." He pulls the kitten from his shoulder, and each paw leaves a trail of thread. The pastor holds the kitten out to Degan. "Take him."

Degan holds the kitten in his lap, and the thing starts in on his hands with its teeth. "Shit!" he says, and tries to push it off, but the kitten latches on to Degan's leg. "Ach! This thing is filthy!"

"Yes," the pastor says, leaning back on the couch and scratching at his hairline. "We're all filthy, Degan. But Jesus loves us still, and he makes us new. What's causing you all this pain?"

"I don't know," Degan says. "I go to work. I come home. I watch TV. I sleep. Ach!" Degan's leg is bleeding freely, and the kitten is content to bat the cap of a Tylenol bottle across the floor.

The pastor smiles. "I want you to take Monday off. I want you to come to the beach with me and my wife."

"I don't know," Degan says.

"You should go, D," I say. "Get some air. Get a change." Degan knows I dive for trash on Saturdays. He does not know about the bomb. "It works for me."

"And you should come too, Matthew," the pastor says. Matthew is a lawyer's name. Everyone calls me Matt.

"Would you come?" Degan asks. He's got a child's voice sometimes, high and pleading.

I do not want to spend Monday with the pastor and his pretty Savannah wife, five months pregnant and already trying to mother the pastor, the eighty-some-odd congregants, and anyone else who sticks around too long. I'm not the kind to put a person in a box, but if she were a bird, she'd be a gull. I had dinner at their place a week ago, Degan and I both did. It's part of the pastor's plan to build the church—have all the church workers around the same table. The yard crew; Ramone, Paul, and Franny; the office lady, Susan; and the "outreach department," Degan and me.

"I'll have work," I say. "Monday is a good day to visit the nursing home."

"No," the pastor says. He's at the height of his powers now, leaned forward with one hand on his knee and the other rubbing Degan's back. "Come. Fellowship is the heart of it all," he says.

The kitten is back on Degan's lap now and back to biting. Degan knocks it around with his hand and strokes it down its back.

"You want to take that to the shelter?" I ask. "I'll drive us."

"No," the pastor says again. "We'll wash it."

***

The first time I came over to Degan's and found him on the couch with his folder out, I asked him to come fishing with me. He said no, but he did seem interested in the how of it. How I fished. Did I let three or five lines off the side of the boat and sit, like a spider, in the middle of them waiting on a bite, or did I let one off and wait with my forefinger on the line, like a trigger, to sense any bumps or nibbles, to feel the lead weight dragging slowly across the bottom? Or maybe, did I use a spear? I told him I just dropped a line over the side and watched the tip of the rod. He seemed disappointed by that.

"How do you do it?" I asked. We had never fished together before.

"I don't," he said. "I wouldn't want a hook in my sandwich. Have it jerked through the side of my mouth."

"Me neither."

We watched some cable after that. We made soup in Degan's kitchen—that's when I first found the gun he keeps tucked behind the spices. Degan is a half-decent cook and had a good bit to say about how the soup should be made, what should go in and how much.

"Why'd you want to cut yourself like that?" I asked while I seared chunks of chicken breast and he chopped celery. "Got this place near the water. Got your health. This cherry gig with the church." We made out OK from the pastor's little job. Not lordly living, but good enough.

"I don't think this life matters much," he said.

"Whatdya mean?"

"I cook the chicken. My body uses it up, I have to cook another tomorrow. Again and again. What for?"

"For whatever you want."

"I don't know what that is," he said. "And anyway, you believe in God?" Degan slid the celery slices into the pot with the back of the big chef's knife. He could filet himself a hundred different ways in this house. Anyone could, really. Filet themselves. But we don't.

"I believe enough," I said. "I don't think it's nothing when it's over."

"That's it, then!" he said. "That's how I feel too. And these holy men and pastors and nuns and superiors, they're on to something. That many people can't be wrong. That statue they got in Brazil, the Jesus statue that's a thousand feet tall, all the people that made that can't be wrong." He was dicing an onion now, and lost in his own voice, looking down at the vegetable and at nothing.

"All those pounds and pounds of brain thinking for thousands of years. We don't know what comes next, but it's something. Maybe it's better—if the part that knows about what's next can feel and know more than the nerves and the brains and the fingers and feet. Shit!" He had knicked his finger, and blood ran to the knuckle. On the onion. On the knife. Degan washed the cut in the sink.

"Sure," I said, and dropped the chicken into the pot.

Degan was looking for something to wrap his finger in. He picked up a rag—too dirty. He picked up a napkin, but it bled through in a second. He pulled a hand towel from a rack in his little bathroom.

"We'll find out eventually," I said. "Whatever it is. No rush."

"Yeah," he said. "I just want to know. I get bored."

"It can wait," I said. "People need you here. All the Brazilians and pastors and the pamphlets." I knew he liked the tract pamphlet job. I'd seen the way he'd light up when he got a hold of some nonbeliever. "Don't you want to know?" he'd say to them at the bus station or on the street. "Don't you want to know what kind of kingdom is waiting for you? What comes next?" He made his voice all crazy when he said it. Like his son was missing. Like his son was gone. "What comes next!?"

***

The pastor catches the kitten by the scruff and gets himself cut in the thick of the thumb. While he's pressing a paper towel to his hand and looking under Degan's sink for the hydrogen peroxide, Degan drops the cat into his kitchen sink and hoses the thing down with the faucet gun while I try to drizzle dish soap on its back and not its eyes. The kitten is making terrible noises. Alien yowls and half-formed hisses. It keeps trying to climb out, and I keep pushing it back into the sink with a scrubber-on-a-stick. I try to rub in the soap with the scrubber, but the kitten just savages it. Some dead fleas fall off, and the water circling the drain is brown, but, in any way that matters, we do not wash the cat.

"When you start the day like this, with changing a life, you can't help but feel better, eh?" The pastor rubs Degan's shoulder with his unbloodied hand while I fix a clean paper towel to his cut hand with some painter's tape. Seems half of ministry is back rubs.

"How do we dry it?" Degan asks.

The kitten climbs out of the sink, shivering now and pink skin showing through the thin white fur.

"It'll lick dry," the pastor says. "Do you have a cloth bag?"

"No," Degan says.

"They love to be in bags."

"I just have trash bags," Degan says.

"That won't do."

We decide to lay one of Degan's shirts overtop of the kitten and scoop it off of the kitchen counter like that, where it can roll around on the floor. I can't help but think of the grainy footage of burlap sack beheadings.

With the situation somewhat contained, the pastor ducks out, saying he'll see us Monday around nine.

Degan and I sit on his couch and watch the kitten throw itself at Degan's booted feet.

"You can't keep calling me like that," I say.

"Yeah," Degan says.

"If you need to talk, I understand, but don't call and hang up."

"Yeah."

I look around the apartment. There's the little coffee table littered with Christian lifestyle magazines and empty glasses with milk rings in their bottoms. There's the tower of CDs in the corner. There's the picture on the wall of Degan's family—a mother and father and three kids coming up to their parent's knees. I've never met any of them.

"You gonna be alright?" I ask.

"I'm gonna be alright," he says. There's a Rocky marathon on TV. We order Chinese.

***

The thing about people is they're worlds, whole worlds, underneath those fleshy brows and knotty skulls. You don't know what they're going to do. If they mean what they say. What they *really* mean when they say it.

I wake up to the phone Sunday morning just in time to hear Degan click the line dead. When I get over to the house, he is finishing the kittens, cutting the last one's throat and bleeding it into the grass behind his townhouse. The other two cats lay in the grass like soiled rags, and Degan kneels among them with the blood-smeared cordless phone nearby.

"D," I say. "Shit, D."

"I'm sorry," he says. "I'm sorry. I was bored." He sounds like he's sleepwalking.

I take the folder from his limp hand, and lead him upstairs by the arm, where I wash his hands in the sink. It's a strange thing to wash another person's hands. Looking at them, lathered and bloody in the sink, and your hands moving over them, the brain can get confused. You almost think they're your hands. You can almost feel them.

I rinse out the coffee pot and fill it with cold water. I push Degan by the back of the neck until his head is over the sink and pour the water over his head.

"Cold," he says.

"Yeah." I refill the coffee pot and pour it over him again before I sit him down on the couch and dry his head with a towel. "You did a bad thing, D," I say.

"I know."

"What should I do?" I ask.

"Call the police, I guess."

I sit down next to him on the couch. "Why did you kill them?" I don't know what I want him to say. That, what? He was bored of living, bored of them living. That he was going to beam-them-up-Scotty one at a time so they could take part in the glorious after and then follow them, like a goddamn crazy.

"It was them or me," he said.

"No," I say. "It wasn't."

"It was," he said.

"D."

"It was, it was, it was. I swear it. I swear to God."

"What do you want me to do," I ask. "Call the police and have you locked up? You gonna kill someone next?"

"Maybe."

The day my father ran into the dumpster, he said something like that. I was thirteen, oiling down my bike. Getting the chain so that it glistened and ran like water around the chainwheel and cassette. Spinning the tires with the thing flipped over on its handlebars and savoring the click-click-click-click. He came down the stairs with a jug of orange juice pinned to his chest like a purple heart.

"Go inside," he said.

"I'm working," I said.

"Go inside." We knew the score, the both of us. He liked to drink, and I was on a big self-righteous kick about it. I'd steal his truck keys regularly when he got home from work. He'd get pissed and start keeping them in his pocket. I'd get pissed, get his truck up on a jack, and take off a tire. Hide that. Eventually he got to where he promised me he wouldn't get snouted up and drive. To make the promise stick, he would surrender his keys to me whenever he got home.

"You going to drive?" I asked, even though I had the keys in my pocket.

"No." He was leaning against one of the stilt pilings of the house and trying his best to stay upright.

"Do you want to drive?"

"Maybe."

Before the tow man could remove his wrecked truck, I peeked through the mess of the crushed cab to see how he'd done it. A new key was jammed into the ignition, shiny and fresh made. Kids are dumb.

I stay the night on Degan's couch, watching him and thinking about what to do and not coming up with much while he sleeps like the dead. The next morning, I have him shower while I throw away the kittens and call the pastor.

"We won't be able to make it," I say.

"Ah," the pastor says back. "Ah, why's that?" And Degan must have known I'd call or else snuck the cordless into the bathroom with him. I should have watched him. Should have made him shower with the curtain drawn back. He gets on the line saying "No, no! We'll be there! Count on it!"

We ride to the pastor's in my truck, and I try to focus on the road and not how fucking sideways this has all gone and is going. Despite everything, it feels strange to be off on a Monday, the streets mostly empty and the beach bare. I can see the morning gray-beige of it flashing at the end of the roads that split from Ocean Boulevard and run down to the sea. The pastor's house is right on the beach, a big three story affair with a Spanish tile roof and a nice porch overlooking the water and the sand. Drying towels wave from the railing. The windows are open wide. It's fall and there's a pleasant breeze about, blowing sand and orange leaves around the road.

"Why do you want to do this?" I ask.

"Could be good," Degan says. "I believe in God."

I don't know what to make of that. "We'll stay for a minute," I say. "But then we go back. Go talk to someone." I look over at him, and he's staring out the window that faces inland. "Get you some help, brother."

"OK."

***

"Come on in!" the pastor's wife mouths in the driveway and waves us in, waddling to the car before I can even get the thing parked.

"Morning, Mrs. Dresden," I say.

"Come in, come in," she says, and starts back to the garage. "And call me Cher."

The house is stilted, and beneath the whole of it, the pastor and his wife have set out wicker chairs and big steel fans. There's a ping-pong table and a punching bag. There's a refrigerator of Coke and bottled water, the pastor's favorite sin. I had spoken to him before about getting paper cups and a water cooler for the church instead of a big iced bucket of plastic bottles, bottles and caps that, invariably, find their way to the street, the beach, the tide. He said he'd give it a think.

We sit around the kitchen table with the pastor and Cher, having some kind of brunch. Fried tomatoes and pita chips with pimento cheese, each of us chewing carefully and commenting on anything we can see. A painting of a sea turtle. A collection of torpedo-shaped olive snail shells, each covered in coffee-colored patterns that look orderly enough to read. I figure we can eat, and then I'll think of some way to get us out of there. The stove left on at Degan's or some shit. I'll figure out the rest as I go.

"Boys," Cher says. "I need your honest opinion. Does this baby make me look fat?" We all make a sociable laugh, and Cher laughs the most, fingertips laid over her gently bulging belly, where a screen-printed, blue-eyed baby peeks eerily, as if from a tent. "Hi!" a speech bubble connected to the shirt-baby reads.

"We're all excited to meet this guy," Degan says. "Thank you for having us."

The pastor looks pleased by this. "Whatever happened to that kitten?" he asks.

"I kept it," Degan says.

I look across the glass table that the pastor and Cher have pulled up to catch all the light coming from the sun over the ocean, and Degan is looking the pastor straight on with the light of Christ in his eye, and this feels different than my father now. This feels like: "What the fuck?"

"Got it living in a box downstairs with its brother and sister," Degan says. "Some food out for them."

"Shouldn't keep them down there," I say. "Coyotes around."

Cher groans. "Mercy."

"They're not all bad," I say. "It's not pretty, but feral cats do more harm. Kill everything. Coyotes'd prefer moles. Rodents."

"Well those kittens got claws," the pastor says, and holds up his scabbed thumb.

"They're fighters," Degan says, and I'm looking at him and the scratch marks across his hands, and he's not looking back.

We finish up the tomatoes and make to head to the beach. That's when I pull my move. "Dang it!" I say. "You know, we left the stove on at your house, D."

"Oh gosh," Cher says. "Run and get it. It's just a mile."

"We should."

"No, I know it's off, I know it. I turned it off myself," Degan says.

"No, I know it's on," I say.

"It's not," Degan says, and looks at me like: "It's done." He flips me his house keys. "Go check if you don't believe me."

I look back at him, and he doesn't flinch. I look away. "Let's go to the beach."

***

The pastor and Cher lay out a big purple blanket, Degan carries an oversized umbrella, and I drag a cooler of plastic bottles and ice. It's a little after noon now, and the beach is filling up. Retirees with folding chairs that strap to their backs and coolers with chunky sand tires. Women with children too young to be in school—and a few who probably should be. A gang of liberated dogs sprint in front of the surf.

"It's not too bad," the pastor says.

"No," I say, but I am watching Degan and he is watching the beach. The children. The dogs. We've worked together two years now. Shared meals. Smelled each other's farts. When my little brother came unhinged and had to stay for a while, Degan made him feel at home. We grilled hot dogs, hamburgers, shrimp, watermelon, whatever we could fit on my grill, we'd grill it. Every weekend for two months. I don't know what I'm going to do. I've got the feeling that I'm watching him in a riptide, and he's just letting himself get pulled out to sea. He's floating on his back even. He's spraying water from his mouth like a little fountain. What the fuck?

Cher scoots close to the pastor and the two of them sip bottled water and read their books, her in the sun and him in the shade, while Degan and I sit out on the edge of the blanket and toe canals in the sand.

"You don't have to do anything," Degan says to me, so just I can hear. The dogs on the beach have learned they can swim. A boy and his father have joined them in the waves. "I mean, it's not your shit."

"I know," I say. "I know that."

"But you're gonna do something."

"It's a little my shit," I say.

Degan looks at me, dirty blond hair in his eyes and a raggedy hoody on over jeans rolled to his knees. A half-beard dripping off his chin. He looks like a kid, and we're the same age. He looks like a kid, but he's thirty-three years old, and he could kill himself with anything on this beach. He could just bury his head in the sand. I can't stop him. I can't watch him every day. It's hard to watch him now. But we're connected, him and me.

"I'm not happy here," he says. "I mean, what do you have to look forward to?"

"You don't want a family?" I ask.

"No."

"You don't want to work with the church anymore?"

"It's fine," he says.

A squeal turns all of our heads down the beach. One of the dogs is having a squat in the water while the man and boy laugh crazy.

"We're salesmen for something people can make at home. Make for free," Degan says, still smiling at the shitting dog. "Everyone has their own idea of God already, and we're all going to meet it sooner or later. Everyone gets to see what's behind the curtain. I know something's coming. I'm tired of talking about it—about God. Sorry to be dramatic," he adds. "Sorry about the cats."

"Is that why you did it? Sent them behind the curtain?" The both of us are looking out at the water, and my stomach turns when I remember distantly, like it was years ago, him kneeling in the blood and the grass.

"I wanted to know if it would matter. If, like, I would feel further away from God or closer or anything at all. Like, if that didn't matter, what would?"

"Hm." I see the lighthouse over the horizon, and I know the bomb is close. No boats are bobbing around in the water. The Atlantic is calm, rolling between blue and gray. "Did you feel anything?" I ask.

"I felt ugly. I felt a hundred miles high."

I stand. "Come on," I say, and peel off a sweatshirt. "Strip the jeans." I start walking for the water.

"Where are you going?" Degan asks. "Water's freezing now." But he's pulling out of his pant legs as he says it. Balling up his hoody.

"You're going to want to see this." I look back, and the pastor and Cher are watching us. I think about nuclear fire washing over them on the beach, blowing them into nothing and burning the beach into a single sheet of glass. I'm glad it hasn't happened. I wave, and they wave back.

"What is it?" Degan asks.

"It's a nuclear bomb," I say. We hit the water and start wading out, and it is cold, but not too cold. It's warmer than the air. We're getting pushed back by the waves and making up ground on the ebb, hopping the swells and then paddling out deeper. Degan is a smoker and starts coughing and sucking in water with his air. We're out pretty far. One waves slaps us. Another turns us over.

"Your gonna drown us," Degan says. He'd follow me anywhere.

"Keep swimming," I say. I don't look back to see if he does, but I can hear the kicking of his feet, how he brings them way out of the water and slams them back down. It goes thunk-thunk-thunk in my ears as they pass in and out of the water in the course of my strokes. I stop to tread water and rest, watching Degan struggling in the light chop that has begun to fin around us. We're over a hundred yards from the shore, but I can still make out the pastor's umbrella with ease. Like a rose-colored pimple on the cheek of the beach, which glows yellow-white in the high sun. Degan reaches me, blowing and wheezing. I swim out a few yards more and then stand, the water reaching my thigh.

Degan laughs and bends at the waist to suck air into his lungs. There are sandbars like this all over. You have to know where they lie. A little farther out, I see the Styrofoam float I use to mark the bomb bobbing up and down.

"You ready?" I ask.

"Yeah."

Beneath the surface, the ocean is grainy and green. Flecks of shell and sand and whatever else sparkle in the light cutting down from above, cutting down in clean, white bars from the sky. The water here is silty. A mess. You can't see past a few feet most places. I follow the little float's cord with my hand until I reach the bottom and see the rust-brown hulk of the bomb, half buried in the sand, spotted with barnacles. A glass bottle rolls some feet away, as if summoned.

I lay my hand on the bomb and feel the rough of its body. Above me, Degan kicks wildly, trying to tread, before he shoots back up to the surface and reappears, pushing down to the bottom and the bomb and me. I wave for him to come closer, to feel. He touches the bomb with his hand and has to swim back for more air. He motions for me to come with him, but I can hold on for a while longer. And, anyway, I want him to feel the dive alone. To feel the sun and the air on his cheeks above the water, and then the pressure and chill of the ocean when you force yourself down to the bottom. I want to watch him lay a full hand on the bomb when he has earned it with the air in his lungs and the meat in his legs. I want him to pass from the cloud strewn overworld of promises and uncertainty into the foggy underworld of salt and secret knowledge—that there are consequences for the things we use and throw away, for the things we do. That any second, this behemoth could wake and transport us all to a different sort of place that, in our bones—in *both* our bones—we know exists and is sustained by the instinctual nothing prayers of millions. What is God, if not a behemoth like that? I want Degan to know and to feel the secret of this bomb and the lapping film of the ocean's surface: that this too is a curtain.

FEATHER BOUNTY

Emu are excellent swimmers. I didn't know that until today, when, after screaming from a switchback in the Smoky Mountains for Perry to "net it! Net! It!" I watched the runaway farm bird shrug off the cast net and dive into the Black River. Like a fish it dove. Into water that can put a shine on granite and sweep a tall man off his feet. Like an enormous, flightless fish.

Perry howls. We watch the fluffy mass and periscope head move across the river, white water dragging at the body, pushing it downstream, but then the strong legs find ground and the bird is up, up and out of the river, airing stubby, flipper wings, shaking the plumage of its tail, gazing over the river at Perry with its blood orange eyes.

Perry picks up a stone.

"Hold!" I call, but he's already hurling. The first falls short. The second too.

The emu trots into the trees. It picks scaled feet over roots. It climbs the stony embankment with the ease of a goat and not at all a bird of the Australian plains—or even the high piedmont of Georgia, that hilly land all bunched around the heels of the mountains.

This is our third day on the hunt for Annabelle, emu at large. There's no price on her head, but Perry figures there will be a reward. I've told him I know a man who will give us five dollars per feather. This is not true, of course, but it was enough for Perry to pick up any we've come across on the trail. He is fifteen and in the strange middle ground. Young enough to be fooled by my feather bounty, old enough to be suspended for boning behind the geometry trailer. "Five dollars," he says every time he finds one.

There are feathers littering the ground at the river bank where we came upon Annabelle preening herself. "Five. Five. Five." Perry slides them into a Ziplock and stows them in the brain of his forty-liter pack. We have enough kit for one more night.

"We can't return the bird if you stone it," I say when I get down the slope.

Perry is taking off his heavy boots and lashing them to his backpack. Next he'll slip on his river-crossing shoes—a pair of Crocs I bought ten years ago for a trip in the Rockies. Perry had been small enough that I'd simply carried him over whatever we'd needed to cross. "I just wanted to give her pause," he says.

"Give her pause?"

"Yeah. Make her stop so I could get another throw with the net."

The cast net is draped mercifully over a rock though the river makes its snatches. The steel weights along its edges have snagged on something. Perry can't pull it in. "Better grab that net before you lose it," I say. "Only have the one."

"I know it," Perry says. He wades out, slips and wets himself to the chest, finds his feet and makes it to the net rock, coiling up the throw line before he makes it across the river, zagging from rock to rock. Pink mound. Green mound. Blue mound. Bank.

I'm standing on the far side next to his pack, getting my own water shoes on. "Good," I say. "Now come back across and get your shit." Too much, I think. "Get your stuff."

Perry drops the net in the mud. "Really?"

"Really," I say. "River's too deep for me to cross with both."

"Just carry it," he says. He begins that short-step pace he adopted at ten or so. Back and forth along the bank. "I'm not going back across just for the bag. I got the net."

"You threw the net. You wanted to be the net man. Now come back for your gear."

"No," he says.

"Perry," I say.

"No."

Fifteen. Every interaction is a test. "You're going to sleep in the dirt if you don't get this kit," I say, and start wading.

"Wow." Perry says. "Maybe I ought to lose my learners permit in the river too. Then you'd really be screwed. Who would drive you then?"

"Pardon?"

"You know, because you don't have a license. Because of your DUIs."

A crowd of pebbles have found their way into my sandal, packing into the arch of my foot. Pressing into my heel. "Are you done?"

"I'm sorry," he says. "Sorry. Just get the bag, please. I'm already so far."

"Yeah," I say. I step back to the far bank. Shake the rocks out of my shoe. Heft the bag.

"Thank you," he says.

"Yeah, baby," I say, and hurl the bag toward Perry. Something snaps around in my arm wrong, a tendon or something, but the pack tumbles pretty through the air, end over end. Once over, twice over, then the Black eats it whole. The Kelly Green nylon soaks dark.

***

Over the fire, Perry has three young birch trees arched and tied. Overtop of this, he has draped his sleeping bag. Smaller sticks hang his socks, his spare underwear. His boots are propped like browning marshmallows at the edge of the flames.

"You're gonna melt that sleeping bag," I say.

"Will you just shut up?" he says from the other side of the fire, but he feels the bag to check. A little water drips out where he touches, hisses in the ember-bed.

"Don't be sour," I say. "Emu can smell sour."

"You literally threw my stuff into the river."

"Yeah," I say. I'm cutting a face into the birch limb I've been walking with, working a nose out of a knot. There's still an hour of light left. I'm wondering how long the timer is on Perry's mood. Before long, he pulls his sketchbook from the emu feather bag and starts scratching something out.

I think to check my phone for a text from Kara, but I know I would have felt it buzz in my pocket. Besides, the rules. Rules we'd come up with for these trips, Kara and Perry and me. No phones, unless in emergency. If you want a picture, use your sketchbook. If you want music, sing. If you want to talk to someone, write them a letter. There had been more trips then. Almost every school break. Since Kara and I split, there's been less of it. But the old foundations are still there. This is what we do. When other families were scrounging to drive to Orlando and stay at Disney's Magic Kingdom or taking force-smile photos in front of the Hard Rock Hotel, we were backpacking in Lamar Valley. We were paddling the Savannah River and sleeping on the sandbanks that form in the bends, finding a little wonder and taking our time. I was always proud of that.

"Did you have to fight anyone in prison?" Perry asks over his sketchbook.

"I never went to prison," I say.

"You went to jail."

"That's different. I was alone in a big room for a night. That was it."

"But you got your picture taken? In front of the lines and holding the sign and all."

"No," I say. "They don't make you hold the sign." I reach out my birch limb to him. "Look at that." The face is a long one. A wizard with deep socket eyes and a drooping chin.

Perry examines my work from his spot by the fire. "Good." He has on one of Kara's t-shirts. He recently discovered they're the same size. "Will you go to prison next time?"

"If I get another DUI, yeah," I say, and pull the limb back, begin unpacking my kit. "Anything else you want to know?"

"Really?"

"Sure."

"How old were you when you started having sex?"

"Older than you. Maybe eighteen. Seventeen. I ran with a churchy crowd."

When was it really? I think. Fumbling around at twenty with Kara's friend, Gigi, who would later call things off to study abroad. With just two musketeers left, things with Kara changed for the better. Then the slow crush of jobs and the dumbing lull of comfort and both of us letting things get a little out of hand with the drinking until Perry came and Kara straightened out at a pace I couldn't follow.

When did I have sex last? Six months? Eight?

"Straightedge?" Perry asks.

"No. Was that your first time? At the school?"

"No," he says. "Be funny if it was though. I think I'd rather lose my virginity in gym. Or astronomy. Maybe in the flipped over satellite dish. With the sky projector on."

"Could be nice," I say. I wonder if this is what it should look like. How it should be. My son and I, chewing the fat over a fire. Like old pals? The talk is fragile. Different from before. From: "Go there. Do this. Good."

I strip my shirt and climb into the river, picking my way around the points of rock until I can sit in a hollow. The water is spring-fed and prickles my shoulders into gooseflesh. Cold washes the ache from my legs. Leaves them tight and new.

Perry follows with his sketchbook. I can tell he's drawing my head over the river.

"You going to show me that when you're done?"

"Nope. It's in the rules." Which is true. No one has to show their journal.

I dunk my head. Scrub my face. Dunk again and walk from the river. "You want to know more about the jail thing?"

"Not really," he says. "Just that Mom doesn't tell me much."

"That's so you don't worry."

"Does that make any sense to you?" he asks. "Like, if I never told you why I got suspended, or like, when I would go back to school, or why I was failing, would you worry less?"

"I don't worry about you failing," I say. "I do worry about you getting someone pregnant."

"Why?"

"Because you're too young to join the Navy."

"No, why don't you worry about me failing?" Perry rips out his sketch and fires it. Little scraps of ash-paper drift up in big, witchy swirls, riding the air, collapsing on the drying socks.

"You're going to pass," I say. "You're allowed to mess up once. You just have to turn the boat around now."

"Yeah."

"Right now, you're just where you need to be. You're suspended. You're in the woods. You're recharging. You'll be in new classes next year. Maybe a new school, if you want. You're going to turn it around."

"Yeah," he says. "I'll start the water for dinner." He leaves his sketchbook on the ground, walks to the bank with our cook pot and the pocket stove. The cover opens in a breeze and a crooked ink Kara stares out with cross-hatched shadows covering one half of her face like a veil, washing her lips and chin.

I flip the book closed. Weight it with a stick.

We've covered some ten miles today, down a thousand feet to the river and then some ways alongside it, riding the gentle up-and-down of the earth. Perry has a smear of mud running from his sock to his thigh. His face is red and streaming in the humid air, makes the thin sheen of a beard on his face, pools to his chin, drips away. I wish I was good enough to catch that with a pencil.

"Yellow rice tonight?" I ask. "And tuna?"

"Sure," he says. He washes the pot in the river, fills it. Starts the gas hissing. Lights it to a burning growl.

I settle into a cigarette and let my eyes close. I dream of all the things the emu will do for us when we come upon it drinking downstream, scooping the water with its beak and sort of hopping it down its throat.

I could pick a path through the woods that brings us up behind the bird, silent and clean.

Perry would step in front to hurl the net from a ledge of pines, and it must be that Annabelle wants to be caught because once the net is over her, I see her just plopping down and waiting to have a little leash put around her neck before she walks, tame, back to camp. We eat yellow rice and tuna and take turns drawing the gray, alien neck that weaves, snakelike through the air, snatching mosquitoes before they can bite. We marvel and laugh. We tell the story to each other and then to everyone we know. We talk about this for years.

I push the edges of the dream, and Kara calls. The woman whose carport I crushed is settling out of court. The magnet school calls. It was all a misunderstanding. Of course Perry can come back. New evidence has come to light.

But in reality, I turn to see Perry scrolling through his phone at the riverside, the cookpot flipped upside down in the dirt. We are never going to catch this damn bird.

"No phones," I say.

"It's Mom," he says. "I can come back to school. Just have to write an essay."

"Great news."

"Yeah."

"What's the essay about?" I ask.

Perry is still tapping his phone, waiting for Kara, who's tapping on the other side. He lifts it to his face. Smiles. Gives a thumbs up. "Sex," he says. "Why I shouldn't be having it." He laughs.

"What's funny?"

"Just sort of stupid, right? Like, when I finish the essay, by the time someone at the school reads it, it'll be the end of summer, and I'll be sixteen. The age of consent. So like, all this boo-hoo essay will be like, 'I'm so sorry. I do solemnly swear not to have sex,' but it'll be legal."

"I don't think it's ever legal to have sex at a school," I say. "Maybe write about that."

"I'm reading this book on sex therapy. *The Deed* by Amita Kapoor. She says that restricting sex to the bedroom is the death of discovery. The thing is to follow your shared intuition."

"Well," I say. "You can get arrested for that too."

"That's what I want to be, a sex therapist. Helping people. Talking about stuff," Perry says. "I'd put Georgia somewhere in the late fifties, sexually. You know sodomy was legalized in 1998, but there are still people in prison? It's like ground zero here."

"You're doing sodomy?" I dig the bag of Rice Sides from the bear bag and toss it to him.

"Just one bag?" he asks.

"It's family-sized," I say. "Does your mom know all this? This sex stuff?"

"Yeah," he says.

"What does she say about it?"

"It's science. What can she say?"

"Yeah," I say, and prepare the plastic camp bowls. What did I want out of this trip? To try and crack this rock in my gut. Tell Perry I'm sorry for being the one calling the house phone from the police station asking, "Can you pass the phone to your mother?" while someone shouts behind me that the officers can all go to hell. "Sorry, kid," I guess I could say. But we're already so out of context— the context being the three months I spent in rehab and phoneless, getting a regular letter from my mother and a handful from Perry saying something stiff like, "Dear Dad, I'm so glad you're getting help. I'm so glad you're going to meetings. I'm so glad you're going to be better soon," while everyone in the facility told me how lucky I was to be there. And to hear Perry now, talking this sex stuff. Asking me what he's asking. I know it: he didn't write those rehab letters.

I open my sketchbook, flip past two sketches of Perry in his hammock yesterday, his toes poking over the fabric like the heads of nervous, scouting soldiers. I start a letter:

Son,

> *Tomorrow we'll catch this emu. I don't know how we'll get it back to the farm. The car's too small. We'll probably have to call and see if the farmer will come out to the trailhead. Come to think of it, I don't know how we'll move the thing at all. I heard they kick like hell.*
>
> *What else?*
>
> *I'm proud of the reading you're doing about the sex stuff. I'm sorry for the drinking stuff. I don't think sodomy should be a crime.*
>
> *—Dad*

I rip out the letter. Burn it up. Perry's socks are too close to the flame, and I pull them away. Flip his sleeping bag on the birch trees, which is not going to dry before dark. He can use mine, I think. I can lay in the open air of a hammock. So long as it doesn't rain.

"Rice is done," Perry says.

I blow the dust and crumbs out of the plastic camp bowls and fork in the lemon-flavored tuna. Bring them to where Perry is stirring the little rice pot, steaming on its collapsible stovetop. He has filled our water bottles with Black River. They're glowing yellow-brown from iodine. Stinking and safe. "Twenty grams of protein," I say, mixing the bright yellow rice with the pink tuna shreds. "Emu hunter's feast." That earns something. A smirk.

***

That night, we lay in hammocks strung between the pines. The glowing hands on my watch face say it is nine o'clock. Bugs drone around my face without fear of death, by spray or crushing force. They're all sexed up and ready to go. They need my blood to lay their eggs. "Bugs getting you?"

"No."

"What's the secret, doctor?"

"Got a net on my face."

I lean forward to see Perry with a ball cap and head-net pulled over that. He has a flashlight clipped to the brim of the hat and his sketchbook out. "What are you writing?"

"A letter," he says. "I'm sorry for yelling today."

"That's okay."

"It was dumb." Perry's headlamp goes dark. "But you know what you were saying earlier about turning the boat?" he asks. "Well it's like, I don't think my boat needs to turn. It's like, I like my boat."

"I meant the suspension and the grades," I say. "But you don't have to read it to me, the letter. It's in the rules."

"It's okay," he says.

"Okay."

"It's like sometimes you need to perform dad stuff."

"What does that mean?" I ask. "I'm your dad."

"Right. So just say what you normally think about, and not the turn the boat around stuff."

I'm thinking, I can't see a single star. It's all pine arms and pine hands. The wind comes off the mountain, brushing through the trees overhead. I'm not getting much of it to cool my sweating face. Whatever air is moving, it's moving high up there, cooling the birds at roost maybe, but not the meaty land walkers like me. Like me and Perry and this emu. "I bet that emu is hot," I say. "We'll probably see him in the parking lot, trying to thumb a ride to town. Get some AC."

"Well, she's Australian," Perry says.

"Well, it's winter in Australia right now."

"I don't think that matters," he says. "Are you dating anyone?"

"Not a lot of people to date at the facility," I say.

"There wasn't anyone you liked? Someone you would look for whenever you got into a room, someone you hoped would be the same place as you, someone you thought about?"

"No," I say. The truth? There was a dozen. "I hung that part of me up."

"For how long?" he asked.

"Whenever. It's not a time thing. Whenever I get this drinking stuff sorted out."

"When will that be?"

"I don't know."

"What do you do when you're not going to meetings?"

"I'm at work."

"What about when you get home?"

"I'm at home. I cook dinner. I watch TV. I may get a dog, then I'll walk the dog. What do you do when you get home?"

"I walk out to the road and catch rides to town. Go to the park. There's a girl, Lisa."

"Good."

"Yeah," he says. "Do you think you're honest?"

"Honest enough."

"What does that mean?"

"Sometimes you have to measure what you tell."

"Why?"

"Because it might hurt people."

"But you still did it," he says. "The thing that hurts."

"Then you shouldn't do that thing." The air is cold enough to drift down now and pick up the clean river smell. I feel the sweat on my cheeks lifting away, turning to air. "Did your mom tell you what happened before I went to the facility?"

"She said you broke into a house."

"Something like that."

"Do you know why you did it?"

"I was angry. A woman said some nasty things about me on the internet."

"Were you drunk?"

"Not really."

"Do you feel better that I know about it? Like, it's not a secret anymore. And I know more about you now. Like, the real you."

"Not really," I say. I'm thinking of the things the woman said on the internet about me and getting mad again, thinking I should have made her post something saying she was deranged or senile or something, thinking how nothing ever goes away, and the beauty of these backpacking trips is in their isolation. In the absence of specific memory. In objectives.

There are two thousand feet of elevation to gain. There are boulders to be scrambled. There is the hanging of hammocks. The cooking of meals. The sanitizing of water. The struggle for dry feet. And if the truth of "what I do when I get home" was naked and plain, I might just end it and send a text like that to a woman, like, "I'm just going to end it" until I send it a few times and she posts online that I'm sick and suicidal and anyone who knows me should reach out, and I look like a crazy man, and I have a drink, and I drive my car to her house, through her fold-down garage, kick a door until it breaks, take her by the arm and shake for her to "take it back," those things she said where anyone can see. And who would want their child to see that? All the thousand, thousand pieces of things like that. Even if they are the truth. What good do they do? For him to know. For Perry.

***

I wake first and listen to the world warm up. The Black River comes to a dead drop here, a short one. I can hear the crash of it falling and getting sucked into a hydraulic where the rocks wait. It's been falling and sucking all night, but for some reason, I can only hear it now, drowning the footfalls and morning talk of people on the trail, the skirmishing of squirrels, a woodpecker tearing loose a chunk of bark.

I leave Perry sleeping in his hammock. I don't know how he sleeps through the morning, so bright. He's diagonal in the sack. His hat has fallen off his head in the night, but it's still trapped in the bug net so it looks like a misshapen fish beneath his face.

A couple of butterflies swirl and flirt while I boil water for coffee. Fifteen miles or so away, where the river grows wide and slow, our car is waiting. I can't drive it. Perry and his permit will get us home. Get me home, anyway, where Kara will meet us and take Perry off to write his sexual manifesto for the superintendent of schools.

I hear a gunshot down the trail, a short crack. Then another. I walk down with my wizard-face birch limb and find out what's what before long. Two men have gone off trail, sliding down the loam ridge to stand over a clump of gray feathers in a pine bottom. One of them has a rifle. The other picks at a gray leg as long as mine, and jumps back when it kicks loose. The rifleman shoots the emu. Then he shoots it again. It's a .22. That's a lot of bird for a .22.

"Hey!"

The rifleman waves. "Brained it!" he shouts. He claps the leg man on the shoulder. "Bet you never seen one of these."

Closer, I see the emu's head has been good and shattered. There is a small hole in the high neck. There are two more through the eye.

"Hated to dirty that eye," the rifleman says while I have my look.

"I was hunting it too," I say. "Was going to net it."

"Net it?"

"Yeah," I say. "My boy and I."

The rifleman grunts. "Good thing you didn't." He shows me a wax paper tag attached to a metal twist tie, the sort you buy in-season and attach to a deer. "We're the only emu hunters out here," he says. "Bonafide." He and the leg man might be twins. They have long brown button ups on. They each wear snake boots to their knees. "How would you move it anyhow?" he asks. His partner is making a slit in the emu's leg, slotting the tag behind the tendon.

"How are you going to move it?" I ask.

"Got a four-wheeler. Up-trail. You at the site nearby?"

"Yeah."

"Sorry for the shots then," he says. "We went to cross there then doubled back when we caught sign."

"What sign?" I ask.

"Looked like it had come down for a morning swim," the leg man says. "Didn't know they could swim."

The men drag the bird through the ferns and up the ridge then down the trail. A lot of blood follows.

I pick up a clean feather and pocket it, wondering what I'll tell Perry. It doesn't seem like the truth would hurt. The bird was loose, and everyone knew it. There were jokes about what kind of damage it might do, but nothing too serious. I hadn't expected anyone would kill it. I guess I expected nothing would be done. That it would just be this funny thing that people talked about from time to time. Annabelle the emu, Georgia's favorite fugitive. There'd be sightings, but everyone would just sort of gasp and laugh or whatever. Eventually, maybe they'd make t-shirts and patches. We'd all see the emu pass into legend. Now I wonder if it'll even make the news. A brain-shot emu isn't quite as funny.

At camp, Perry is still sleeping. I left the stove burner on and the water has bubbled to nothing, leaving a pot that screams when I scoop it in the Black. I mourn the emu over instant coffee and oatmeal, praying that Perry sleeps a hundred years and feeling the moments between now and when I'll have to tell or not tell him burn away.

From over the lip of the hammock, my boy's leg snakes out. The toes trail the ground. Next comes an arm, and in the hard angle of the morning, I see the golden hairs that cover it. Before long, he'll emerge. With whatever progress he can make in his run of things, with whatever visions of honesty, with whatever ideas he has of me; he'll come down. But in this moment, before he has pulled the bug net off his head, and before he knows that Annabelle was killed, and before we hike out of these mountains—before all that, he will lift his head above his hammock and scan the ridgeline beyond the Black River. He will be looking for the world's second-largest bird.

TV for People

"Who's a good boy?" the TV in Karl and Dee's den asks. "Who is it? Is it you?"

Karl and Dee are out, so it's just me and the dog.

On the TV, a woman's face is filling the screen and smiling. "It *is* you! It's *you*! Good dog! *Good* boy! *Good* girl!"

The dog is sleeping on my lap and does not seem interested in the woman on the Dog Channel. Not as interested as I am anyway. She has dark skin and a spray of darker freckles that look like seeds above her sunflower dress. I wonder how she would look on TV for people. Like, would she wear a different dress, or would they use different lighting? Has this lighting been approved by a panel of veterinarians? A panel of dog psychologists? A kennel? Did they walk this woman, in this dress, through a shelter and say, "This is our girl!" when the beagles stopped their baying and Rottweilers laid down and played dead?

I slide the dog off my lap and walk to the kitchen. I pour a glass of water from the sink. Then another, while I look at the pictures Karl and Dee have hung around the room.

There's Karl and Dee at the Grand Canyon. And here's Karl and Dee at the National Mall.

Dee has left me a list of to-dos. She knows I like that kind of thing, to feel a part of things. To help out, even on vacation. I'm the kind that likes a task.

First on the list: *security beepers*, and next to the list is a plastic bag of the beepers that we picked out yesterday—the sort with the little magnetic strips that scream like hell when the door opens. Right in your ear, they scream.

I take a bath in Karl and Dee's bathroom and treat myself to the rainbow spread of conditioners and soaps until I smell like a movie star in the Amazon. Then I see about the beepers. I've got them all set up with Velcro so Karl can take them off the doors if they piss him off with their screaming, but Dee can put them up when Karl goes to work early and she's home with the dog.

The dog is not going to be much help with intruders. It's a ratter, Dee says. Bred for chasing vermin into holes and tight places. It might be confused with a pair of rolled up, wooly socks.

Next on the list: *Lambchop haircut*, and there's a number to call the groomer. Also, Karl has told me where I can find some clippers in the house.

The dog is standing on my shoes in the kitchen, and it seems docile enough. When I was small, I was given jobs like this, at the animal hospital or for our dogs at home. Standard procedure was to tie the dog to a trailer hitch and buzz it down. Give it a wash afterward to get all the stray hair, but those were all outdoor mongrels. Big beautiful bastards we'd found or the shelter had found or that some old lady owned but couldn't wrestle to the trailer hitch herself.

I call the groomer, and a woman answers. She sounds sweet, like the sunflower woman from TV. She knows the dog by name.

"Do you have the Dog Channel?" I ask.

"We keep it on in the lobby."

"Ah," I say all disappointed. "We've been working to limit this girl's screen time. I just wish she'd play outside."

"We have a yard," the groomer says.

"Well, that could work." We make an appointment for two.

The list ends after *haircut*, but I know there's a pile of glass out on the sidewalk I'd like to sweep up. This kind of stuff, you'd have to drag me to back home, where it's *my* glass all busted up and spread over the sidewalk, and it's *my* neighbors having to either walk out in the street or up in the grass to get around it when they do their morning jogs or walk their kids or dogs. But here, I love it. I can pretend that this is my home and my city and my neighbors that wave from their porches and come over to chew the fat. And being in a new place can gift you that—the chance to be someone better.

"You're new?" a neighbor asks.

"Oh, no. Just down for the weekend," I say. "House sitting."

And the neighbor gives me that good neighbor smile and that good neighbor shake before they come out with a glass of tea and that good neighbor glow about them like, this is a neighborhood that cleans up its shit. This is a neighborhood that gives a damn, even though the streetlights are shot out and the stop signs are shot up and there's that one truck with the tires flattened that's sat around for so long, ten generations of squirrels have crawled from under the hood.

A man in a ripped coat and a beanie comes shuffling down the street, and the neighbor and I stand like a wall.

"Good trees here, though," I say, all sage and connected to the soul of community.

"Ayuh," says the neighbor, and we down the tea while the dog noses around in the leaves. These are the kinds of things that get sweeter when you're far from home.

A kid goes by on a bike, and the streets look wide and friendly, and I get the idea to take the dog for a walk. There's a park a few blocks away.

We set out at a healthy clip, but soon the dog is sitting down and trying to smell this or that and otherwise not walking, so we camp out for a while and take in the day. The dog has a big dreamy look on its face, all tuckered out in the grass, and I take a picture to send to Karl and Dee. They'll probably hang it in the kitchen. I take a few more with the camera imposing this or that on the dog's face. A set of rabbit ears. A monocle. A Western style mustache and two six shooters.

I stop at a gas station for a cup of water for the dog and a couple beers for me. We drink in the shade of the oaks behind the station and walk home swinging the world by the tail.

***

In the guestroom, with the dog sticking its paws under the door, I make my noontime webcam with Bethany, 21, Florida. And this one's a humdinger.

Bethany, 21, Florida has on a heavy winter coat and the comments are piling up asking her to "take it off, darlin'," or else wishing they could "rip that zipper, baby," and Bethany, 21, Florida is playing the game and acting like there's something off camera she would rather be doing and talking about all the normal things she has to do that day. In today's fantasy, she has O-Chem in an hour and has been cramming all night, and "aw shit, the heat's out again, and it's so cold."

Dr3amBoat86 tips ten credits, and the comments explode in smiley faces and tongue-out faces and dollar-sign faces as Bethany, 21, Florida tugs the zipper down to show that she's wearing a Japanese sailor costume underneath before she pulls the zipper back up to her chin.

A guest spews that she's a tease, a few more pile on. Dr3amBoat86 and I suggest they adjust their manners.

Dee calls my cell.

"Have you fed the animal?"

"Presently," I say. We talk about the beepers and the Velcro and how, no, it's no trouble at all.

Bethany, 21, Florida has the coat off now, and I can tell she's got the usual mix of tunes going because she's kneeling on her computer chair and playing with whatever toys she's brought for today's show.

I see the shit-bird commenters are tipping their usual shit-bird credits, while the fly-by guest viewers scream for more in capital letters and exclamation points. Dee is going on about the fruit in the refrigerator, and I kick in a full thirty credits.

All I can hear is Dee telling me where the dog's poop bags are, but on the screen, I can see the muted, pale face of Bethany, 21, Florida saying my name and sliding out of her top.

"I'm stepping into the shower," I tell Dee. We make plans to meet Karl for dinner when he gets off.

Bethany, 21, Florida runs through her routine, and I do what I meant to do, stepping into a place that's not Dee and Karl's house or the good neighborhood; a different place, where a transpacific sailor was washed from the deck of her cruiser, picked up by a barge, transported around Cape Fear, and limped her way up to Florida, where she's changing for organic chemistry and making love to a disembodied, purple version of me she has fastened to the headboard of her twin-long just before she has to run out the door—which she does.

I shower and take the dog to the groomer, feeling springy.

In the reception area, people stand with their dogs on short leashes. I check in with the groomer, who may or may not be the woman I spoke to on the phone. She's short with short hair and a nasty bruise sliding out of the sleeve of her scrubs.

"Just a little off the top for me," I say.

"What?" she says.

"We're the two o'clock." And I see she remembers me now because she smiles and nods to the TV hung in the corner of the room while she checks us in to the system.

"You're Karl?" she asks.

"Yes," I say.

"You can wait, or we can call your cell."

The Dog Channel is showing a fifties-style mailman deliver a stack of letters to a house full of barking dogs. The frame cuts to another camera inside the house, zoomed in on the mail slot that spits out the stack of letters and shows the dogs peaceably milling around in the pile. The camera cuts back outside, where the mailman is petting a dog and laughing, all Andy Griffith and apple pie.

A long-haired Chihuahua wears a muzzle and gurgles like a mad man when the dog and I sit down across the room. The owner, a guy in a cap, tugs the loose skin of the Chihuahua's neck, and the dog gurgles on a little quieter.

Two women with matching collies sit looking at their phones while, somewhere in the bowels of the shop, a dog cries.

Dee and Karl's dog is sitting in my lap, straining to see if the collies might want to play. They do, and the three bounce around in the play area until it's the collies' turn to be groomed and, together, they're led into the back after a very naked German Shepherd comes out with its body bent around its owner's leg.

The man in the cap and I watch the Dog Channel run through possible scenarios a dog might encounter at home. A crying child. A stompy, grabby child. A child that likes to eat on the floor. All while the Dog Channel dogs lounge about and smile with their tongues off to one side. Hollywood dogs, like a glossy picture of the real, hot-breathed thing.

I keep waiting on the sunflower woman to appear and give me some words of affirmation, but what I'm imagining is fine: the sunflower woman and I lying on a picnic blanket somewhere, a proper church picnic blanket that's thick enough to muffle out the rocks, and there's a bluegrass band playing somewhere that disagrees with us, so we gather up the dogs to go. And just as we're hooking them all in to their leashes and knocking them off of one another and calling goodbyes to the other folks on their similar picnic blankets, and I'm slipping a collar on a big yellow lab, the sunflower woman lets a kiss like honey drip from her mouth to mine, and her face is fever flushed.

Karl and Dee's dog makes a run at the Chihuahua, and the man in the cap blocks it with his foot, not kicking it, but pushing it back in a way I don't like.

I pick up the dog and stand over him some. He's not an especially big man and his dog has a muzzle and I want him to know that it's not OK to push another person's dog with his foot.

"Keep a hold on that, huh," the man in the cap says from his seat. He's got a face like a bulldog, rolled over and sad.

"Watch the foot, pal," I say.

"Just keep a hold on it." He doesn't want to talk about this, I can see. He's got one of his hands in the pockets of his ratty army jacket and the other wrapped around his dog. The Chihuahua is quivering in the way that all small, cornered things do. "And sit down," the man says.

"I'll sit when I'm ready to sit."

"Problem?" the groomer woman asks, and the man in the cap says no, and I say no and sit down, and we pretend that each other doesn't exist until the groomer calls for "Stacy," and the man in the cap carries the Chihuahua up to the counter and goes out for a smoke.

What kind of name is Stacy for a dog? I think. I watch the man in the cap smoking outside the door. He has his back to the door like a chicken shit. I imagine all the things that spiral out of that kind of man, the kind that smokes cigarettes and pushes a little wooly thing like the dog around with his feet, even though I, myself, smoke cigarettes and once, after he called me something I didn't like, kicked a boy on a soccer field when he was down. I think these things, too, to make it clear to myself that I know the kind of man the man in the cap is.

In the parking lot, there are just a few cars. There's the one I'm driving that looks like a white beetle and there are two other beetle-shaped ones that I guess belong to the groomers, and then there's a truck that, I just know, belongs to the man in the cap, and I imagine all the things I'd like to do to it. Piss in the AC intake so that the filter soaks it up like a sponge. Slip a knife into the back left tire, so he doesn't find it until he's on the highway. Kick a dent into the tailgate so everyone behind him in traffic knows, and thinks to themselves, "there's a poor, redneck chicken shit who can't afford to pop out a dent."

The groomer calls for the dog, and I, still scalding, haul it to the counter while it squirms. Behind the groomer, I can see Stacy, the Chihuahua, still muzzled and tied up to a little stick, tight so it can't look around or lunge, while a man buzzes the shaggy hair from its belly.

The groomer at the counter carries Karl and Dee's dog back somewhere I can't see, and the groomer with Stacy sets down his clippers and walks away, and, outside, I see that the man in the cap has walked out of view, and I imagine the little window I have for justice. I imagine the camera of the Dog Channel following me as I slip behind the counter and approach the stainless steel table where the dog is leashed up. I imagine the snarling and the whimpering and the piss that pools at its feet before running to the central drain.

Rough stuff like that. I can imagine it all without getting a knot in my stomach. Not because it's what I'd like to do—to hurt this dog because of its owner's bad attitude—but because when you're righting a wrong, you have to harden yourself to these kinds of scruples.

The man in the cap checks his phone outside the door. Then he walks out to his truck. He rolls down the window and hangs a cigarette out.

There's a dog on the far side of the parking lot, a long, ropey dog. Ropey in the spine, with bunches of fur all down the line of its back. Weird looking dog. Snuffling around the gutter that runs off the strip mall. Chasing something now. A toad that's making mad hops around the building side, trying its damnest not to be lunch.

The man in the cap gets out of his truck, and he starts on a line for the ropey dog, and that gets the blood into my shoulders quick. "You see this guy?" I say to the groomer behind the register, but there's no groomer there. They're all in the back shaving Karl and Dee's dog down from a wooly pair of socks to something slimmer.

On the television, the sunflower woman appears in a field of lavender, no less. The blooms rise to her hips. Dogs are running in the background, so many I think they must be computer generated, but then they're jumping all over the sunflower woman, who laughs and pushes them down and says "sit now" and delights in the quick compliance of the dogs—labradors and labradoodles and doodles-

full-on. Standards, those are called. And all I have to do in the world is sit here and wait on Karl and Dee's dog and consider the sunflower woman—if she's real and what she does when she's not in this field, which may very well be a green screen in Atlanta. But there's the option of more.

The man in the cap is almost to the corner of the strip mall where the ropey dog disappeared after the toad and the option has been extended to me to act. Possibly in violence. But the ropey dog, what can he do? What choice is he going to be given when the man's boots are stomping for his skull?

I see the man in the cap has left his truck door open. He was so ready to go bash this stray, he left the keys in the ignition. I take them out. There's nothing attached to them. No chains or other keys, just the bare silver hardware store copy that slides easy into my pocket. It's always a strange thing, to be in a new car, especially someone else's. There is so much of them left inside. In the man in the cap's truck, the smell of dogs and stale tobacco and hot upholstery. There's a cigarette box graveyard on the dash. At least ten empty boxes with their lids flipped open. Twenty cigs per box, I think. Two hundred cigarettes.

Inside the glove box is a revolver in a clip holster. It's loaded. I clip it on my belt. In the crease of the seat are pumpkin seed shells. In the floorboard is a crate the right size for a Chihuahua. What kind of bastard keeps his dog on the floor?

The ropey dog and the man in the cap haven't reappeared from the side of the strip mall. No one has come out of the groomers to say, "Your dog is ready," or "We've already called the police on that man in the cap. Whatever he's done to the ropey dog, there was nothing you could do. Go on and come back inside. There's someone we'd like to meet you." And inside would, of course, be the sunflower woman, who was always as real as me or Karl and Dee or anyone. But no one comes out to say that, and I can see the counter is still empty, so the option is still there. The option to do a little right.

Around the strip mall, I don't see anyone, man or cap or dog. I have the revolver out of its holster and it fits my hand just fine. The little cuts in the plastic grip hold on to my skin tight and the weight is comfortable. I'm seeing the world through iron sights. The whole world behind the bead at the end of the barrel, but there's only so much to see. Just a little drainage ditch where the water runs off the side of the strip mall and into the grass and some cattails with brown fuzzy tops where the mower man halts his mowing and the still rain water makes a little pool. There are mosquitos in the air. There is a little worn path that goes back into the woods behind the khaki concrete of the mall.

"Hey there!" I call into the woods. "Ropey dog!" But there's no reply. I follow the path into the woods, where the sun can't breach. Spanish bayonet plants spread themselves out at the feet of twisted oak trees, and the moss hangs into the eyes of the birds who hop from limb to limb, looking me and the revolver up and down. Deeper in the woods, I hear barking.

My phone is buzzing against my thigh. When I check the screen, it's Karl. "Hey," I say.

"I just got a call from the groomers," he says. "They say Lambchop is done."

"Sounds good," I say. I have the revolver trained on the path ahead, waiting on the man and the dog. "I'm just down the street. Took a walk."

The thing about Karl is that he never takes any chances. Someone called his office once, some deranged somebody, and told him he ought to leave five thousand dollars in his mailbox if he didn't want his house to burn down.

What does Karl do? He calls the police and reports the whole thing. The police send a cruiser to Karl's house. They try to find out who called the office, but, of course, they can't. Karl sits up in bed at night with Dee and his little sock dog and a baseball bat by the foot of his bed—like he was going to grand slam the Molotov cocktail right back out his window.

Karl and Dee are petrified. The police tell them, "Don't worry." They tell them, "These things happen." And they'll keep happening. If you're not willing to take a chance and undergo a little danger to do a little good, then you know what happens?

"What happens?" I ask myself. "Nothing," I answer.

The fire insurance scammers get away and call someone else in a month when things cool out. The newbies in the online chats keep on skimping on the tips and clamoring for big reveals. The man in the cap keeps kicking dogs. Keeps spitting pumpkin seeds inside his truck, while his dog sits caged on the floor. Keeps after this old ropey dog in the Spanish bayonet woods.

I slip down through some hanging vines, and soon there's a creek to cross. I roll my pants and step stone to stone, no sweat. On the other side of the creek is a switch grass meadow, and in the meadow is a whole lot of nothing, but the ground is wet and soft and holds the shape of your foot when you pass over.

I search for sign of the man in the cap or the ropey dog and find it. Find the presses of his boots alongside the sharp cuts of deer and the shallow pads of dogs, the clumps of scat, the twisted ropes of fur from coyotes and the curly-q smoothbore turds of wild turkeys and the pellet shit of rabbits and deer.

All over the meadow I search for the true line of the man's boots with the revolver held out in front of me until my arm tires, and then with the revolver down at my side until my hand begins to chafe and the sun slips under the high tree line and the sweat wets the front and back of my shirt from the tracking and worrying about the ropey dog and the man in the cap escaping and all the bad he'll do. All the bad he'll do if I don't find him and take the chance that I've been given to do a little good and clean up this town and make my small difference in the world, which is the charge we all carry, but carry especially when we're in a new place. When we're the stranger that comes to town.

Dark comes and my phone buzzes again for Karl, but I click it dead. It buzzes again and I throw it aside in the grass. Might as well lose the thing if it's going to buzz all night, I think.

The thing about Karl is that he doesn't understand the difference in right and wrong. There's the wrong way: There's cowardice and letting others do for you and waiting in bed for your problems to come roaring onto your carpet floor or lie shattered on the concrete in front of your house. And there's the right way: There's going out and doing for yourself and for others that can't do. There's energy and the willingness to confront chance. There's Bethany, 21, Florida in her sailor's uniform or her moon boots and fishbowl helmet or her white scientist's lab coat. There's the sunflower woman, easing out of the television screen in homes all across America, speaking to the few who she knows will listen, who will cock their ears to the side and consider the message she's offering. The affirmation. The sunflower woman who affirms me and strokes the hair along the ridge of my skull and says, "Yes, you know what you're doing. Yes, there's good to be done."

I slide the revolver back into its clip holster. I use the sky to find the edge of the meadow, where the oak canopy crowds out the stars and the forest is dark with opportunity and places where the man in the cap might hide. I call for old ropey. "Good boy," I say when I hear the jangling of his collar bells somewhere in the deep.

Black Bird

Patton stood at the sink and looked through the eyes of a fox. The mask was one of his favorites, a Celtic design of light, carved wood. Its deep etchings were charred black: the tip of the fox's nose, the slender lines beneath the eyes. Flanges of red stained wood jutted six inches above Patton's head where they ended in the sharp, alert points of the fox's ears. The mask tapered to a clever chin, and below that, a short wooden dowel had been attached for easy handling.

The world narrowed through the thin cuts of the fox mask. It had been one of his first acquisitions. A souvenir from days gone by. Patton had a dozen others more ornate displayed in a converted bedroom of his previous home, but the fox he always kept in the kitchen; it was easy to take down and talk about or pass around. The fox was resilient. Patton imagined the mask pulled tight against his face with animal sinew. On a night raid. Men and women draped in furs and moving close to the ground, legs like springs beneath them. He pushed the fox against his face and found he could not breathe. It was, after all, a replica.

In the back yard of his new home, the vultures filed out of the utility shed like dwarves, two small ones first, then one as large as a kindergartener. They did not make to hunt or take off or pick at the dirt for worms; they only tottered in the sun. One hopped and made a few ugly flaps to reach the roof of the shed, which sagged like a paper hat in the rain. The largest bird sat at the head of the driveway to bask. Then it jumped to the hood of Patton's car.

"Out!" Patton shouted from the open garage. "Go!"

Patton picked up a stick and threw it at the base of the car. Next, he whizzed a shoe over the roof. A rake poked from an oil drum of yard tools, things left from the previous owners, and Patton slid it from the barrel.

The vulture addressed him from atop the Chrysler's oversized grill, tiny skinned head tilted and wings outstretched, the black flight feathers flashing their ivory underside. It was almost pretty, in a certain way. In the way all things are pretty, Patton thought. In a symmetrical kind of way. He could see daylight through the nostril hole in the beak.

Patton replaced the rake and took up the garden hose. Reluctantly, under the spray, the vulture jumped from the hood to shuffle back to the shed, walking bent over, like a man with his hands in his pockets, driven by a strong wind.

Patton followed with the hose, backing the bird into a corner of the shed where it was content to look away and weather the hose, hunching and, every now and then, picking up its feet. The smell hung heavy in the dark of the shed; shit and rot and the sticking sick that follows cheap, wet wood. Patton sprayed the mud floor, hoping for a concrete bottom but making a gurgling hole. He turned the hose back to the vulture. The water on the feathers made a hollow noise. Patton wondered how waterproof the bird was. It was not, after all, a water bird. It was an altitude bird. A soaring kind of bird. He imagined the soft under-feathers soaked through and chilling against the skin of the vulture's chest. If it were winter, that might kill. Men had been killed that way, wet and left to freeze.

A fourth vulture dropped down from the rafters of the shed, and Patton screamed and jumped back. Cussing, then laughing in the rush of fear, he pressed his thumb over the mouth of the hose, driving the water in a hard, tight jet. But the birds only turned to face the corner, showing Patton their hunched backs and knitting their wings one over the other. He let the pressure off the hose, and the birds stood dripping, still facing away with their bald heads low like henpecked old men.

The remaining vultures watched from the yard, bored.

***

Patton stood again at the kitchen sink, glaring out at the yard and letting cool water run over his hands and wrists. He splashed his face and pressed his hands over the sockets of his eyes. The fox mask laughed from the wall.

This was his third week in the house, and the charm of the Stratford Yellow bricks was waning. Since leaving his wife and selling off anything they shared, Patton had spent his nights in the motels stretched between Athens and Commerce, while the majority of his belongings lay piled in his sister's house. After a month of storing Patton's boxes in her bedroom, it was decided that Patton should buy a new place.

The house went for peanuts at auction due to damages. A tree had come through the master bedroom and still lay there, quietly turning to dirt. The elderly owners had been out at the time, Patton was told, and had fled to Florida. Now the bedroom sat like a government test site behind thick sheets of plastic that dripped from the humid air. Patton slept in a guest room and didn't give the damage much thought. Maybe he would leave it, he had joked to his sister. Plant a garden.

The phone rang, and Patton's ex-wife, Julie, came wheezing into the line. "The fox isn't with the rest of them," she said.

"It should be," Patton said, feeling his eyes drawn to the mirth of the fox face.

"I fucking know it should be. And I think you have it. And I'm going to come get it, if I don't find it in my mailbox tomorrow morning."

"Check around some more before you get all riled up."

Patton dropped the call and took the phone off its plastic

receiver. He wondered how Julie had found his number. Even he didn't know his number. He made a mental note to call his sister, who was still a Catholic and believed in reconciliation, even now. The last time Patton had spoken to Julie, it had been to retrieve his belongings from the house. Some clothes. Picture albums from his mother. They had spoken through a mediator because the last time Patton had seen Julie it had been through the cracked windshield of his Chrysler Imperial, and she was wrapped around their neighbor, Jeb. Patton had driven through the bedroom wall. The "rare and valuable" mask collection was at the top of Julie's list of demands after that. And it was worth thousands.

"I don't know why you're surprised," Julie said when he confronted her about the affair, days before he drove into Jeb's house. It was true that Patton had been gone most evenings and that he often left early for flea markets or trade shows, places where masks could be found. And he was no stranger to infidelity. Nor was Jeb the first "spare," as Patton and Julie called them. Patton and Julie had fallen in love as young people, and, the fact was, they were not young anymore. They were too old to be squeamish about what they wanted. They kept the spares quiet. It was part of the new sort of thing that their marriage had become. But Jeb?

Jeb was a deputy sheriff pushing fifty, and had, once, been a sort of friend. He whined often of his bachelor's status, all the near misses and heartbreak burnouts and whatever side-show he was rolling with. He would spout this at any opportunity: whenever he came over to the house for drinks, on the odd days when he and Patton would go fishing, over the backs of pews at church.

"Mary May," he once whispered over Patton's shoulder at the ten o'clock service.

"Shut it."

"She comes with these cleaners, May Day Maids, they're called. Except they do more than scrub your floors."

That Christmas, Julie had the idea to invite Jeb over. Their family was small, no kids and one parent apiece. They had room.

Jeb came over and got too drunk before lunch. Patton had to take him out to sober up.

"Pull it together," he'd said while Jeb swayed over the mint plants that Julie grew around the side of the house.

"Julie's mom. You think there's a chance?"

"Hell no," Patton said.

"Put me next to her at dinner. I'm lonely, Pat."

No one called Patton "Pat".

Around the table, Jeb fawned over the mother, making what slurry conversation he could. "Say, Pat," he said. "Say, these faces," he rolled his head around at the tall African Goma masks hung around the dining room. "What's the deal?"

"I just like them," Patton said.

"Why?"

"They mean something. Everything about them meant something to the people who made them. The details. The little things that made a man feel like an animal. Or a god. More than a man."

"You ever put them on?"

"No," Patton said. "They're exhibit pieces. Art."

Jeb leaned back on the hind legs of his chair, sniffing the large ovals cut in one of the masks. Making a show of it. "*Someone's* been playing god in this one!"

Months later, while Patton and Julie were drunk and in a fight over what to watch on television, Julie would reference that Christmas as her first interest in Jeb and "his irreverence."

"And I want you to know," she said. "We wear a different mask every time."

Driving through Jeb's wall felt like a necessity after that. Patton quit his job at the Home Depot—he was retired anyway—and moved out to the barrens of Madison, where his sister lived. To a death-bird boneyard, apparently.

***

The porch of the house had been left with a set of dog-gnawed wicker furniture, and Patton reclined in one of the rickety seats, browsing new masks on the internet and picking at the rusty metal that poked through the arms of the chair. The fox sat in the chair next to him. He rarely bought the masks off the web, there was no sport in it, but he liked to look.

The vultures were holding court in the middle of the yard as evening wore to night. Patton considered shooting them. They were protected by the state, but there was no one here to see, though a small, religious part of him imagined curses and black magic. Egyptian Thoth and his ibis head that could, if desired, look like a turkey vulture.

Two leggy figures walked in the dark behind the birds. One made a chittering, kissing noise—the way some people talk to cats.

Patton stayed still.

The figures were out of view now, but there wasn't much in the back corner of the yard. Behind Patton's lot was a dead river run over with kudzu, a sea of it that washed into his land and, eventually, would swallow it. The house had sat empty for some time before Patton purchased it, and the kudzu had continued its march, unimpeded by Weedwackers and sprays, halfway to the house. A lawn service had pushed it back, but bits of the yard were surrendered.

An oak in the back corner of the lot stood with long tendrils of kudzu hanging from its brain, draping down to the ground like a willow and trailing back to the overgrowth of the back lot. He imagined the figures there, lying beneath the oak and tucked behind a curtain of kudzu.

Fine, he thought.

Longing stirred in him and brought with it the usual highlight reel of bank tellers and cashiers who had smiled at him as they performed their small services—the unacknowledged brushing that happens outside of the formalities of a love affair. And there was Pamela, who, until she left for a trade tour, he met monthly at

Keller's Flea Market—in her manager's suite. He did not think of Julie. Had not thought of her in that way for years. But that did not mean he wasn't thinking.

Somewhere, an animal moaned over the din of the night bugs. Then again. Then no more.

***

In the morning, Patton put the fox mask on the top of his head and called his sister.

"You gave her my number?" he asked.

"You need to talk to her. Just try it in doses," Marcy said.

"Don't give out my number, please."

"OK. How's the house? Do you need Kyle?"

Kyle was Marcy's son, home from college and without much to do. He had helped Patton eat a pot of spaghetti a week or so past.

"No, that's fine. Just don't give out my number. It's not good— with Julie."

"We're, none of us, good all the time," Marcy said. "She had a moment." Marcy was always trying to slip into homily.

"It's done, Marcy."

The phone line buzzed that a call was waiting. It was half past one. Julie should be working.

"I have to go, Marce. Got to get out in the lawn," Patton said.

"You'll burn up at this time."

The line buzzed again.

"I'll call you tomorrow."

On the next line, Jeb's greasy tenor was talking to someone in the background.

"What?" Patton said.

"Pat!" Jeb said. "Look, don't hang up."

"You guys can't call here."

"Hey, I hear you," Jeb said. "It's Julie though, man. She needs that fox mask. You know, lawyers. Rules is rules."

"Oh," Patton said. "If that's all."

"Yeah, brother, that's all." Jeb had taken—what he had called— "all this craziness" hard. Patton could hear the relief in the phone line. Could see Jeb's shit-brown eyes getting all watery, the way they did when he was nervous, or the dawgs played ball, or there was air in his lungs.

"Where was it the last time you saw it?" Patton asked.

"What?"

"When did you see it last?"

"I can't recall," Jeb said.

"Really?" Patton laughed. "Come on, son."

"I don't know."

"Humor me."

"Let the record show, Pat, that I wanted to handle this like men. With words."

"It wasn't too long ago now. You saw it. I think I saw that fox too. I think I saw it strapped to your fat head while you were rolling my wife, you burnout, paper-badge fuck. Check under the bed. Behind the pillows." The phone tore off the wall. Patton had been pushing against it without noticing, pressing until the screws ripped out.

The line was dead. Patton didn't know when Jeb hung up, but he was satisfied. He felt alive. He felt huge and righteous and heartbroke. He felt like he had when, stepping over the rubble that had been Jeb's east-facing wall, he pulled the fox mask from under a sheet of drywall and then backed his big steel car away while Jeb and Julie shouted, hiding their nakedness behind a pile of covers and sheets.

Outside, a dog barked.

Patton pushed the yellowed lace curtains in the living room aside to see a man straining against the leash of a big dog, a lab it looked like, that was snarling and howling at two of the vultures that were cozied up in the bottom of Patton's ditch.

The vultures were watching the dog but not moving.

Patton came marching out of the garage with his rake, waving his hand at the man and dog. "Sorry, there," he said. And then, "Yah! Get!" at the vultures, who seemed more interested in watching the lab getting pulled down the road, still hacking and pulling against the choke chain.

"Get!" Patton said. He pushed against one of the birds with the head of the rake, and it bowed up at him like a goose, taking a step toward him even. That was enough for now, Patton thought, with the man and dog disappeared. He walked backward toward his house with the rake held up like a spear. Then he had the idea to climb into his car and drive it, slowly, across the yard toward the birds.

The vultures stepped aside when the Imperial dipped down into the ditch and stood, inquiring, outside the driver's side window.

Patton honked and revved the Imperial's engine. He tried to back out, but the wheels spun in the patchy dirt of the lawn. He tried to drive through the ditch and the car's long nose stuck into the far side of the ditch, wedging him in.

The vultures pressed the car. When Patton cracked the door to push back, one of the birds pecked at the silver handle.

Patton got out the passenger side and left the Imperial to sit.

***

That night, on the porch again and listening to the cicadas scream, Patton saw the leggy figures crossing the yard again. He had the mask on loosely, so he could lift it to drink and then slide it back down. Patton refilled his glass and wondered after the couple—what things they'd say to each other before they let in to one another. That's what he could never remember, the things that came before. Once in high school, after things were finished, a girl had asked him about children. How many he wanted and what their names might be. That hadn't scared him at seventeen like it scared him now.

It seemed like with Julie, there hadn't been much talk before or after. Their time together was something like a trip to the bank, all waiting and then a bit of well-rehearsed business with everyone trying not to make eye contact for too long. With Pamela at the flea market, they had talked about masks, which she would be getting and which she had sold. She had this nice way of putting her love for the masks and Patton and everything else: "The discovery," she said, "turns me on."

She always had a mask tucked away for herself that she wouldn't talk about—her spare lover. Patton had seen a gold-plated sarcophagus stood up in one of her closets once, behind her winter coats and, studying the delicacies of the metal work, felt jealousy for the first time in years.

A woman's voice, high and sharp, came from somewhere in the dark. It was not a happy sound.

Patton felt he should check it out. A place like this, an old house out in the sticks. Bad things could happen, he thought. Though behind those thoughts flashed boozy images of what he might find tussling beneath the tree. What he might see.

When Patton reached the kudzu oak with the leafy cave, he found it empty. Somewhere past his property he heard voices, and, again, the low moan from the night before. There was a fence where Patton's property ended, and past that, it was a no man's land of strangle vines and hidden ditches. Starved out trees that had succumbed to the kudzu and sunk beneath it to mulch. It was not an easy place to move.

Patton set the bottle by the foot of the oak and, in the quasi-nimble way that some drunks acquire, climbed into the branches. From the height of the tree, he saw two figures and a light some yards away. The light was not sweeping or searching but fixed on a point in the vines, and from the point came the moans.

It would have been impossible to sneak up on anyone through the kudzu lot. Stumping and tripping and cussing, holding the bottle and the fox mask above the tide of brambles and stumps,

Patton made his way to where the light was. "Hello?" he called.

"Here," said a girl's voice. She was no more than sixteen and stood with another younger girl. At their feet, lay a doe with its head propped up under a pink sweater and four inches of yellow-white bone sticking through its leg.

"Oh, gosh," Patton said. His drunkenness shamed him. He set the bottle down, glad to see it disappear beneath the vines, though he was sure the girls had seen it.

"We need to take her to the vet," one of the girls said.

"You shouldn't be out here in the dark," Patton said. "Your folks know you're here?"

"They do," the older girl said.

"Good. Hold this, please." Patton handed the fox mask to the older girl and kneeled by the doe. He could smell the leg festering. Puss had welled up around the gash and bone and rolled down, looking like candle wax dried to the hair of the leg. "You guys did good to find her," he said. "I'll take her to the vet now. I can carry her and get her to my car."

"We can help," the younger girl said. "With the light."

"You know where I live?" Patton asked.

The girls nodded.

"Good. Why don't you leave me with that light, and I'll put it in my mailbox tomorrow? You can come get it then."

"How will you carry her and the light?" the small girl asked. She may have been twelve.

Patton tapped his teeth. "The old miner way. Now, go!"

The girls moved through the lot with ease and before long Patton lost the sound of their passage in the crying of the insects. A thorny locust was perched on the doe's flank, and Patton knocked it away. The deer was barely stirring now. From his pocket, he slipped a fold-out knife, pressed his hand against the doe's head, and slit its throat.

After he moved the doe deeper into the bush and clawed his way back to his own land, Patton shined the flashlight through the pecan trees that stretched out across the yard, looking for the vultures. Empty.

Inside the house, the telephone, sitting in a pile of cords on the counter, was ringing. Could be Julie, Patton thought. Calling to make threats. He thought up something nasty to say to her and picked up the line. Pam's vodka-tonic voice was on the other end.

"There's a Cherokee Booger Dance mask here. Made from gourd and trimmed with fur."

"Pam?" He had given her the number weeks ago, before he even moved.

"It's got a nose like a shlong," she said. The muffled sounds of men and women talking and laughing buzzed behind her voice. Even still, hearing her brought the woolly musk of her apartment and the taste of limes to his senses. She had a habit of hiding them in her mouth before she kissed him.

"Is that why you bought it? The dick nose?"

"I made a bid in New York. I read the Cherokee wore them to scare off demons and prudes."

"I'm spooked."

"Speak louder, honey. I'm at a party."

"That's all hooey," he said louder. "Is the fur rabbit or what?"

"Come see," Pam said, and something in Patton fluttered around.

The bare, plastic sound of a dead phone filled Patton's ears, and he looked to the sink for the fox mask before he remembered it was still with the girl. Fine, he thought.

He walked out to his car and took the .38 revolver from his glovebox.

The doors to the shed were open and had the look of a cave, the aperture jagged and the white barn-style doors hanging off their hinges and gouging the soft ground.

Patton held the gun and light out in front of him. He looked in at the bare, dirt floor. In the rafters of the shed, he heard metal under claw and raised the light to see the vultures, all four of them, huddled together in the low space between the two-by-four trusses and the particle board roof. He leveled the irons on the largest bird's chest. In the close air of the shed, the doe's blood reeked. Patton pulled the trigger and the gun clicked. Empty.

Lights that dwarfed the girl's flashlight flooded Patton's yard, and he heard the roaring of an engine coming up the driveway.

Patton shut off the light and stepped further into the shed with the smell of the vultures hanging like a shroud.

Outside, the engine was purring. There was a knocking and shouting.

"Open up, asshole!" Julie yelled.

The sirens of Jeb's cruiser yelped twice.

Slowly, Patton pulled one of the doors to the shed closed, then the other. From the dark, he could hear Julie beating on the thin metal of the garage door.

"Open up!"

The vultures shifted again in their roost, and Patton slipped the gun into the back of his waistband. He imagined Julie and Jeb circling his house like wolves, checking all the windows, eventually breaking in. He saw them poring through the boxes in his living room and peering through the plastic of the ruined bedroom and snapping to each other to "keep looking" and the two of them searching and searching, and the black birds twittered to one another and scuttled around. Something heavy landed in the mud next to him, and Patton began to snigger. Clutching his ribs with both hands and stifling it all until his lungs were on fire, he laughed.

LAST OF THE BONE-CRUSHING DOGS

As a team, we were broken. The high school football season had ended, and in all ten games, we had lost. At home, they laughed at us from rattling silver bleachers. As far away as Long County and Hepzibah, they aired it out over our heads. They threw the big men up front into the littler ones behind. They ran it down the sideline, where our extras moped and chewed their mouthpieces and swung their heads like cattle to watch their opponents pass by.

We didn't tear through a big sheet of paper at the last home game and stretch out to Ted Nugent's "Stranglehold," because we were locked in the field house, kneeling on the concrete in our clean uniforms, watching the head coach rip his hat. He had forfeited the game after two of ours had been arrested and briefly held for attempted arson. They meant to leave a set of jaws burnt into the enemy's field, but they had stopped to piss in the school's big air conditioning machines and been caught. It was the capstone on a year of cruelty, rebellion, and disappointment.

In the eighties, a live bulldog came to the home games and snapped at the out-of-towners when they passed through the chain link gate, but that dog, Coach told us, had died, and we, as a team, were dead as well. He let the bill of the hat fall to the fieldhouse floor, separated from its cotton cap. He promised a reckoning.

***

In June, we rode three busses to Fort Stewart to practice football for two weeks. Most of the old seniors were graduated, and the power vacuum drew us into the bus seats in a strange way. Normally, we sat in order of ferocity, with the starting, black-penny-wearing boys in the front near the coach, the red-penny-wearing seconds behind them, and the yellow-penny extras in the back, but that day no one wore a mesh penny-jersey on Coach's orders. We sat, cramped in the pleather seats, with bare shoulder pads and athletic shorts in the half-random order we had been clumped by the bus door.

I sat beside Sean Halligan, who was two years older. We were not friends, though we had played on the same teams since Youth League. I didn't take it personally. Sean treated football like church. He had distinguished himself as a weapon, and I had not. We had little to discuss. The boys fought and sang in the rows behind us, but no one kicked the back of our seat.

Coach stood in the aisle at the head of the bus, gripping the seats to his right and left. He spoke, but the chatter kept on until he pounded the metal ceiling with his wedding ring and shouted the last names of the boys in the back who were ramming their neighbors into the windowpanes. I knew it would be Hawkins getting beat against the glass in broad day, or beating one of the rising middle schoolers. Coach moved the super-senior nose guard to the back of the bus, and things quieted down.

"Right now, we're nothing," Coach said. "If you give yourself to this program, you will be more." He was straddling the aisle, staring down at us with his Marine Corps hat and *Bulldogs Football* shirt on—black text on black cotton, a cartoon dog popping a football between its jaws, little puffs of smoke jetting from the nostrils. It was a team tradition that the starting black-penny boys would receive the shirt when the season began. When the coach spoke, the boys in the aisle seats leaned out to stare into his t-shirt, and the boys trapped against the windows stretched out their necks to see.

The big diesel engine buried in our yellow bus sounded like a helicopter's roar when it drove us through the fort's checkpoint, past men with black rifles in their arms. Humvees with antennae bent over their desert camouflage were parked in formation over great fields of asphalt.

In the parking lot, two scales were brought out, and our weights were taken down. While we stood in line, gawking at the military vehicles, I saw the heat roll in like a rain shadow over all our heads.

That night, we slept in stacked apartments built to house military families short-term. I could hear the older boys through the ceiling, shouting, fighting, laughing, while in my sophomore apartment, the lights were out. Four of us shared a room. Hawkins, Peebles, Shae, and I lay on our steel frame beds and pretended to sleep. We didn't want to talk to each other, but we didn't want to go out.

Someone might have said, "I've got cards," but everyone ran a different way when the door to the room was kicked opened and the lights cut on and five junior boys jumped on Peebles to try and tear his nipple off his chest. They didn't have to drag him, they only held him by the shoulders and led him to the kitchen island after the rest of us split.

I ran outside and saw Sean smoking a cigarette beneath a streetlight with three older boys. Inside the apartment, Peebles' shouting was covered by laughter. A black civilian jeep turned into the parking lot and blinded me with its brights. The engine revved and the jeep leaped on the sidewalk. The nose guard leaned out of the passenger window with a squirt gun and shot it into my mouth. A girl squealed in the jeep, and it jerked away.

Nowhere to go, I went back into my apartment and spit on the carpet. The back door was open, and the seniors were gone. I washed out my mouth at the sink. I wondered whose piss it was. Peebles was shouting at Hawkins in our room. I saw him standing over the bed. He was bleeding from the chest, red-faced and throwing straight kicks into Hawkins' back while the other boy curled up and covered his head.

The sophomores resented Hawkins because he wore a chip on his shoulder but was maybe the weakest of us all. At lunch, a senior said Hawkins shit himself on the bus ride, and since then, he had become untouchable. That was the new game.

"I said you fucking left me," Peebles said. He wiped his blood on Hawkins' back.

"Who cares?" Hawkins said.

"Leave him alone," I said. "Take a shower. It's OK."

While Peebles showered, I worked with Hawkins to move one of the steel bunks against the door. Hawkins had noticed that it opened into the room and could be blocked. He chattered about the rubber-tipped feet of the bunk and how they would dig into the carpet and not slide.

"It's an immovable object," he said.

I knew it would only excite the older boys to find the barricade. Something to throw themselves against. I slept on the small couch in the living room, but the stiff government air conditioning drove me back to our room in the middle of the night to get beneath the sheets. It was easy to push the bed blocking the door back a few inches then slide through the cracked doorway.

Everyone was breathing heavily, laid out on their bunks with the fragility of oysters on the half-shell. It made me sick, how easily the lock had turned. All it took was my thumbnail in the groove.

***

The next day after scrimmage, we lay on the ground of the fort's parade field, smelling its toasted, yellow grass. At a whistle, we rose to chop our feet in place. We dropped to the ground. We jumped up again. Late into the day, Coach bled the weakness out with the whistle and the sun, so he said.

Because of a fumble, Sean Halligan was made to run the ball against every player on the team. Each down began with both boys flat on their backs, facing opposite directions, stuck together at the top of their helmets. At the whistle, they rolled to their feet. Sean tried to run past the defender, and the defender tried to tear the ball away or knock Sean down.

Some watched the drill. If there was a breeze, it was possible to enjoy the weather between the up-downs and chopping. I liked to rest my skull against the back of my helmet and search the sky for helicopters, which arrived and departed all day long.

Sean ran past most of us, shearing tackles. I crossed his body with my helmet but couldn't wrap him up. Sixty bodies balled up and thrown at Sean. With every one, he seemed to speed up a little bit. The shoulder pads clacked when they crashed against his legs, but he spun away. The losers ran around the field.

Eight o'clock but the sun wouldn't quit. Coach asked Sean after each collision, "Are you going to drop my football?" or, "Are you hungry for this hit?"

The blow of the whistle and the crack of pads.

"Are you hungry?"

It was Hawkins' turn. He lay on his back with his toes askew, but Sean wouldn't meet him on the ground.

"Can I skip this one? He stinks like shit."

"Hey, Shart!" one of the running juniors called. The chant grew legs. *Shart. Shart.* It spilled over the field. It passed into my body. Fifty teenage boys, like a coven circling the field, straps and buckles rattling, beating their fists on their pads, chanting for bloodsport, chanting for chanting.

"That's not my name," Hawkins shouted.

"Tell them," Coach said. His eyes glistened. He was allergic to certain pollens, which made his sunken eyeballs redden and weep.

Sean had the ball loaded in his arm, tucked against his rib cage safe. If Hawkins were to stand up and take it from him, what could change? What then, Hawkins? Remember the army apartments we will sleep in tonight. Remember the boys in the apartment above ours. We have two weeks to get by.

I wished Sean would just run a little to the side of Hawkins because my mouth was dry and I was tired of running. I wasn't interested in the shit joke or in Hawkins' last stand. He was only drawing heat. Everyone laughed. I began to feel delirious.

"I don't mind hitting you," Hawkins said.

Sean looked at Coach through the dark visor on his helmet. He shrugged.

Coach blew his whistle three times and we rushed to clot in the center of the field. "Bullpen," he said.

We, the black helmeted mass. We, the hateful bunch. We made a circle around Coach and Sean and Hawkins. The seniors slapped Sean on the helmet and called him Irish and Son. No one touched Hawkins, who had rolled over and propped himself into a four-point stance with his legs back and both arms stretched in front of him.

Sean stood casually with the ball, though in the Bullpen drill, he was to tackle Hawkins.

The boys packed in around them. They hung on each other's shoulder pads. Their helmets sat on the tops of their heads, and they chanted a song I didn't know. Something about cattle. Coach was smiling and rubbing his hands like he was about to set down to a feast in the cartoons. I was sure that destroying Hawkins and the rest of us was the shared interest he had hoped to create all along. The fear we were living in at the military apartments was a part of his game plan to revitalize the team. He had told us time and again, an environment of insecurity was the best for an upset. We would do anything to disrupt their system. To break them down.

Then the chant again. *Shart. Shart.* Low and fast and near-mumbled as the circle got tighter. Coach blew the whistle. Sean dipped his shoulder and ran through Hawkins with practiced ease, knocking him on his back.

"Hawkins, are you hungry?"

"Yes, sir." He scrambled to his feet.

"Set it up again."

"Ay there, young Shart!" someone said.

Hawkins slapped his hands on his helmet to the hoots of the crowd, and I watched him go extinct, ossify; never Hawkins, forever Shart. He was drunk on the idea of progress and had come to believe that he had Heart, and that Heart was getting beat down. It was a deep scrape. In sustaining a certain amount of damage, in drawing it out of the team, something was being accomplished.

"Halligan, out. Hoster, in," Coach called, and the backup quarterback took Sean's place in the Bullpen. The whistle blew and Shart was shoved into the mass of pads girding the circle. Someone threw a shoulder into his back and knocked him down.

"Are you hungry?" Coach asked, but it was the team being fed. They gorged themselves on Hawkins' body flopped over, how satisfying it was to watch big Hoster slip the younger boy's sloppy lunge then pancake him. Grind the air out of him. If they could do it here, why not in Long County? Why not in Effingham?

"Meyers," Coach said, and the linebacker broke Shart down.

"Toole."

"Curtis."

"Brown."

They sharpened themselves on Hawkins. They stunted. They took him down with cowboy collars when just a stiff-arm was enough. Someone shot his ankles out.

I tried to circulate the rings of players so that I was never in Coach's line of sight. I didn't want to hit Hawkins. I would never hit him as hard as Sean. Even if I were to level Hawkins, I would be exposed. And if I didn't level Hawkins, what would that mean?

Ollander drove Hawkins into the dirt, and Coach shouted my name. A new chant had started by then, lifting the boys' fists and helmets in the air. They sang, "Where them dawgs at?"

Shart's eyes were wet. Streaks of loose, gray plastic crisscrossed his helmet, and the earth was torn up from the dozen boys who flung themselves into him. He spat on the parade field like an action hero. He got into his busted four-point stance, ass in the air and fingers tilling the dirt.

"Set."

I think it was pride in his eyes, when I took my place across from him. So many times, Coach had said his name. Maybe he was imagining being handed a certificate in the cafeteria at the Gridiron Association's banquet at the end of the year, or thinking *Maybe this one, I can win.*

He kept standing up after he was knocked down. Was he changing into something new? Yesterday they despised him, but today they clapped. Like this was a Christian football movie where, when it was over and we all took a knee to hear Coach say *Today, I saw something I didn't expect to see,* that thing would be Hawkins' redemption, the turning point of everything. It was painful to see that hope in Hawkins because he had been deceived.

He was hyped up, and he had forgotten the sort of cannibalism we were engaged in. He had forgotten that there is an order to these exchanges—that *dog* will always be eaten by *Dog.* He didn't see: Our joint dream of Heart had been perverted, and he had been transformed into a likeness of weakness. He had become a tool to be referenced in the locker room while Coach spoke and the announcers played their music through the big stadium speakers and the visiting team ran warmups on the field.

I've seen a lot from this team. I've seen a lot from the least of you. From the weakest link.

Yeah, yeah, yeah, the seniors sang, elbowing each other, leaning side to side, back to front, on the ones around them. They have never known a win. They are desperate for it. They are ripe with superstition.

"If you give yourself to this team, you will win. Blood takes blood," Coach said on the parade field. "Nothing ever was bought for free."

Shart's leg was shaking over the ground, and I could smell his breath wafting through the split grate of his facemask. One of his fingers is folded into his hand, I guess it was stomped or jammed. And him still thinking, *When this whistle blows, I'm going to pull down some goddamn respect.*

Everyone else knew, when the whistle blew, the black-jersey boys would hold each other by the shoulders and laugh at our tangling. We would collide and roll around, and some would watch and some cheer and others, on the outskirts of the huddle, would stare blankly over the military base, watching the wobbling heat lines that hover over the ground and wonder what comes next.

I was fooled into thinking I was more than I was. I was thinking on Coach's promise, thinking: *I will be more.* This was the foundation we would build ourselves on. I couldn't wait to tear into Hawkins and change things for myself. And Shart like a ladder laid flat on the ground, and his ribs like the rungs, and his eyes like neat holes for my fingers.

SNOWBIRDS

The nights Carey serves at The Ghost, I slip into her place through the back window. I start a load of work clothes in her machine. I shower and shave. I switch the clothes to dry. In Carey's downy covers, I lie awake until she eases through the door and sheds her waitress blacks. Eyes closed, I listen as she drops her skirt at the foot of the bed. Cloth slides on skin as she strips her shirt. Metal clicks on glass as she takes off mood rings and hoopy bracelets, the jangly kind that women wear in twos or threes—Carey wears about ten.

Tonight, I feel the bed sag with her weight and she drags cherry nails up my leg. Her hair trails over my chest. All that yellow hair, down for the night and smelling of cigarettes and Old Bay. When I met her, we were fourteen and breaking into houses like this, snowbird places left empty for the summer, their owners so high in the cotton they'd leave the AC running. Carey had this thing for trying on the clothes. I checked the couches for change and watches. Any ice cream left in the freezer, we'd finish that in the shower and leave the bowls.

Come morning, I make a big breakfast and fix my lunch before the sun's paled the sky. Most days Carey's asleep, but today she's up and drifting around the kitchen while I fry eggs and sausage. She's wearing blue jeans and nothing, playing hellcat lover with the backs of my ears. I ask her what the occasion is.

"Breakfast," she says. She flips a condom into the frying pan, and I snatch it out. Hard old crumbs stick to our skin and we don't stop until the smoke alarm squeals.

I'm still scraping char from the skillet when she comes back into the kitchen, all done up in a dress and her wedding ring on. "Now what's the occasion?"

"William wants to have breakfast," she says. Her heels click on the kitchen tile and she finishes her face in the glare of a framed pastoral—cows chewing cud while a boy looks on. "He's flying in today."

William is a broker in the city. He lives in New York for weeks at a time. He owns a collection of farm art, a thirty-foot Grady-White, Carey's house, Carey's washing machine, the sausage I burnt this morning. I set the skillet down and William grins at me from a photograph above the sink, all six-foot-goofy-four of him. He sits on the crest of a sand dune with his arm around Carey's waist, both of them in white shirts and washed out jeans. "Life's a Beach," the frame reads in cut-out letters. I squeeze Dawn into the skillet and leave it to soak.

Carey wipes her lips with a tissue and tosses it away. "I'll come by later," she says.

The house goes quiet, and I walk around switching off lights. I take a cufflink the shape of New York from the top of William's dresser, the citrus smell of his cologne wafts from an open drawer. I take a pull of Scotch from a decanter in the study. I duck out the window and walk to where I parked, side-arming the cufflink into the marsh that stretches out from William's backyard. A heron takes to the wing without a sound. Beyond the grasses, the ocean is burning. Houses like William's always have a view.

***

At work, I'm peeling shrimp while Martin sings Marshall Tucker to the radio. The season is on, but the trawlers don't go out. Too many years coming up short. Used to be we could fill three coolers with fat-daddy shrimp for fifty dollars and a case of beer—and the old boatmen would leave a trash bag of flounder on top. Now I'm working twenty pounds of crawlers from their shells and dropping them in a bucket and feeling lucky to have them, the whole flaccid bunch, only one in ten are big enough to be veined, and those I just leave be.

Martin and I opened this place our senior year, and the town was good to us. It was a little nothing place on church land—a shack pressed against the highway with the Methodist steeple looming behind. We'd had offers for "better" work—Martin on a charter crew and me at the marina, but this place was ours. People love shrimp. We never needed more.

"I'm gonna find me," Martin sings behind me, eyes closed in song and slashing out trout fillets like a man possessed. Slash. Flip. Slash. "A hole in the wall." He nudges me, but I'm lost in Carey and William over a meal. Probably at the Sunny Side. Probably over coffee, him going on about the firm and his flight and holding her hand under the table and letting his pinky stray up the inside of her thigh. Martin leans back and butts his shoulder to mine. "I'm gonna crawl inside and die." He won't let it go, and I join in. We're on a southbound all the way to Georgia, and I'm feeling all right.

The daily forecast starts to drone, and the bell on the Shrimp Shack's door comes alive. In steps Teddy Long, bamboo cane first and two grandsons after, both of them with buck teeth and hair the color of Tang.

"Mr. Long," I say. The boys hang their faces over the open live well of blue crabs. I wipe my hands to shake.

"You boys have spot-tail?" Teddy's wet eyes are stuck to Martin's work. I bag up six filets. One of the boys reaches his hand into the live well and comes up with a crab by the flippers, leveling it at his cousin. They get shipped off here by their parents every summer. Teddy swats at the boy with his cane. The crab smacks the floor and makes a run for it. The boys scatter, and before I can get around the counter, the crab has backed himself under a bookshelf of charter boat brochures and is flashing his claws to anyone that cares to see.

Teddy shoos the boys out and goads the crab with his cane until it latches on. He drags it out, and I snatch it from the floor. The old man is smiling. Sweat beading up on his brow. "Them boys," he says, and I flip the crab back in the well. He squeezes my arm hard, as if to show he still can. "Carey's looking well," he says, but it's to Martin behind the counter, who mumbles a *yessir*.

"Don't know why she hangs around that Ghost. With all that New York boy's got."

"Can't say," Martin says. "Since we were kids, she's gone her own way."

Long grunts, but there's no story on Martin's face. I hold the door and follow Teddy with the bag of trout until one of the boys takes it from me through the window of the truck. The Longs lurch away and the boy stares me down in the side-view through the rising dust. I just stare back thinking: that's a damn unfortunate-looking child.

A black Mercedes passes the Shack and makes a U. It pops and rumbles over the gravel lot and comes to rest at my feet like an advertisement. Carey and William climb out into the light of day. William beams and socks me in the arm. Carey's smile falters. Hugs all around, and I lead them back to the Shack where Martin comes out to kiss his sister on the cheek. That's when I notice Carey's liquid stride is off, just a hair. She's favoring her right.

"When'd you get in?" Martin asks, and "how long you think you'll stay?"

William goes off talking to Martin about airplanes and big deals. The two of them lean over the counter like old pals, but I see William's not wearing any of his hand jewelry and Carey wanders off to look in the crab well. I ask if she'll help me pick out the oysters they'll want. "Clam's a clam," William says.

Carey just says that "any will do."

Something's been taken out of her. I know it. She's holding her purse with two hands.

William had only hit her once in five years. Things had gotten heated over something, her body withheld or else her job at The Ghost that she'd never give up, not since she was sixteen. Not even when she came home crying after a snowbird put his hand up her skirt and I did four-months in county for cracking his leg with a pipe. Not then, not ever. William had hit her in the stomach before. He'd bruised her ribs. Carey begged me not to do anything. What's he done now?

We all walk out into the sun to see William's Hollywood Mercedes off. I hoist a burlap sack of oysters to my shoulder and take pleasure in dropping it roughly into the open trunk, making sure to miss and scratch through the paint. Right down to the plastic. I hear William curse in the cab. He raises his hand to me behind the windshield, and I try not to stare at Carey through the tint of the glass.

Martin is singing Joplin when I get back inside, his well-sunned arms air-drumming my bucket of shrimp and his Carey-yellow hair rocking all about. I let him be. We close the Shack at four, and I drive the two of us home. "Full moon tonight," Martin says. Over the horizon, the whole white round of it is rising through the still-blue sky. I grunt.

"Could drag a net," Martin says. "Way the shrimp are coming in, we could use it. Score a flounder or two." Martin taps his feet to the radio. I turn it down. "Hell," he says. "S'eating you?" I switch the radio all the way off.

"What did you think of William? The way he didn't have his rings on? And Carey like that?"

"What do you mean? He just got back." When I don't answer, he says, "His fingers probably swole up on the plane." That's Martin: good-enough answer and a half decent song and he's set. "The hell do you mean?" he asks.

"She had a limp."

"I didn't think so," he says.

I turn the radio back on and before long Martin's humming Al Green and staring out the window. I pull up to Martin's house, a one-story brick place under a hundred-year oak, big around as a tractor tire; it had been his parents'.

Martin gets out of the truck and slams the door. "Ride with us tonight. I know Billy and J-Hook will go. J-Hook'll bring his boy. We need a tall man on the end." He's got his arms through the window, and he's talking to me like we're kids again and he needs a ride. I tell him I'll go and putt off through the neighborhood, wishing it were easy as that.

***

At The Ghost, I find Carey in the kitchen rolling silverware in napkins. BA, the washer, is smoking a cigarette in the freezer.

"Check out, BA," I say, and he sulks out the back door.

"What's up?" Carey asks, her eyes a blur between tubs of forks, spoons, and knives, swaddling them in the heavy black napkins with clean, martial sweeps of the hand.

"You tell me."

"Don't play that," she says. "He's home. You know how this works."

"Why were you limping at the Shack?"

"He squeezed my leg. Not a thing you need to worry about."

"When has someone squeezed a leg into a limp?" I ask. "Christ!"

"He wants me to come back with him this time," she says.

"What's new?"

The muscles of Carey's jaw do a little throb and stand up under her skin as she sets her teeth grinding into one another. "I can't do this forever, right? I love it, but not forever."

The first time we made love, we were in this kitchen. Pressed into a pile of wash rags or some other unsavory place that youth allows. Winters, we would climb to the roof and roll our beer bottles to shatter below. But those old things, even the sweetest of them, lose their shine sooner or later. Even ice cream in the shower isn't enough. I can't say why she's stayed this long.

"Do you love me?" I ask, feeling boyish having to say it out loud.

"Yes." The silverware folds itself.

"More than him?"

"I don't know."

I sit down on the kitchen floor and wet my ass in the foam that's run over the lip of BA's sink. There's a run in Carey's tights and I see the patch of hair that she likes to miss under the ball of her ankle. A little stand of dirty blonde a quarter inch long, hiding in the shadow of her bone and begging me not to tell.

"That's just it," she says. "That's all of it."

Out on the floor of the restaurant, someone is shouting that a pod of dolphins has breached in the river. Above our heads, chairs scrape on the floor and the sandals and wedges of the snowbirds crowd to The Ghost's tall, picture windows, pressing their noses to the glass and taking a dozen pictures of the glare.

"You don't have to work here forever," I say. "But you don't have to leave."

"I'd come back sometimes. I'd see you then. And Martin."

Days like this: dolphin days, Carey might make three hundred in tips. Something about the dolphins' gray backs slipping through the brown water. Something about the wild chance that the snowbirds think they're experiencing, like winning the lottery. Like they won, so Carey and her crooked smile and her long curly hair and her little drawl might as well win too. "You win a little, too, honey," they say with their tips. "Because I win, you win. Life is rich. And we're on vacation."

When I worked at The Ghost, BA and I loathed making the long haul to the river each night, hefting trash bags of fish scrap to throw to the tide, but everyone likes the little blow-hole spouts and the drive-by dinner show the pod makes. Everyone likes the dolphins around here.

***

I rent a room from Carey's aunt, a two story dock that they converted into a mother-in-law suite years ago. I'm sitting on my bed and staring at the .38 snub nose I keep under the mattress. I hold it up and sight the marsh. The last time I pulled its trigger, I had the barrel pressed against a big tiger shark that Martin had pulled up to William's boat. The shot had gone straight through. Now I imagine it pressed up under William's head, in the hollow of his jaw. My hands soak the handle. Plans spin circles in blood. We'll have to leave, of course. I have a sister in Charlotte. I can find work. Carey can find work. Martin might come. But the killing. What of that?

I lay back on the bed, gun on my chest, and watch the ceiling fan whirl until it begins to look like the blades are still and the room is spinning. I close my eyes and when I open them again, the room's gone dark. Martin is shaking my shoulder.

"The hell you doing with that gun out? Get your boots and let's go." I stand on wobbly knees. My head feels swollen. I grope for my shoes. Martin takes the pistol from the bed, swings open the cylinder, and swears. "Got the hammer resting on a round. Damn fool." He upends the cylinder over the bed and the bullets hop around like Mexican beans.

"Goddamn, Martin. You could have just knocked," I say.

"We're all family here," William says, ducking into the room. My stomach twists up and I glance at Martin. He just shrugs. "Boat's in the water."

Through the window I see that William's boat is pulled up to the dock. My skiff is crowded up in the corner next to the Grady's bulk. J-Hook and his boy are sitting on a long cooler seat in the bow. Billy Trench is talking to them from the dock. The moon looms above and below, the reflection waving in the water like a flag.

***

The ride to St. Catherines is a short one, but William insists on driving the boat and has to pick his way around the river before we get to the open water of the sound. Martin stands over his shoulder and directs us around sand bars that lay just out of sight. Ten years ago, Martin, Carey, and I ran aground one at low tide, all of us blasted. It was New Year's Eve. Carey cut her head on the edge of my skiff's windshield. A little silver crescent still hangs above her brow. It was damn cold and we covered up with whatever we could find: a fire blanket that smelled of rot and oil, life jackets, the boat's plastic cover. All three of us shivered and cussed and told what stories we could think of until the tide rose enough that Martin and I could shove the boat off the sand. When we got back from the hospital the next morning, I proposed to Carey in her parent's driveway. She cried buckets and said no.

We arrive at the island and Martin passes out smokes to everyone, J-Hook's boy included. We begin untangling the seine net by lantern and moon. William stands in the water up to his knees and pisses, going on about the easy beauty of the sea and how he favors this quiet little life. Billy Trench gets a fire going and produces a bottle of rum.

Each man takes ahold of the net and stretches it out, the weights at the bottom drag crazy circles in the sand. Most seines have just two wooden poles on the ends, like an over-large tennis net, but this is a creation of Martin's and my design. Twice as long as a normal seine and with an extra pole in the middle, made with the long, shallow beach of St. Catherines in mind. Martin, J-Hook, and I walk the big net out to where the water wets our heels. Martin digs his feet into the sand, and J-Hook and I wade our poles out into the surf. By the time we get the thing taut, I'm up to my neck in the black water and Martin is seventy-five feet away. I can see the shapes of William, Billy, and the boy passing the rum in the firelight. The current pulls at my legs.

"Ho!" Martin calls, and J-Hook and I start walking, swinging the seine like a closing door toward land. The trick is keeping the pole pushed down to the bottom. J-Hook stumbles and goes under. He comes up spitting. Someone laughs on the beach, and the net lurches as something big tears under or through it. We've pulled in full grown bass before. Plenty of sharks. Whole coolers of shrimp. All manner of trashfish. Sometimes nothing at all.

We drag the net up on the beach, shake it out, and the pull looks alright. The men on the beach run around picking up the flipping shrimp and tossing them into coolers while J-Hook's boy shines the lantern wherever he's called.

"Damn!" Martin shouts, and the haul's better than I thought. Three-finger shrimp, fat as lords.

We pick up all the shrimp we can see and kick most of the fish back. The next pull is better and the one after better still. We're all a little drunk on the luck of it. Martin overhands a whiting at my head that would have left a bruise. I throw some kind of fish back, laughing until William heaves a saltwater cat at J-Hook, and I remember Carey's limp and the gun. Billy Trench is proper rum-drunk and slips in a scramble for a big flounder in the surf. Martin sings "Fire on the Mountain" and it's good enough to spread, even William comes in on the chorus. The coolers are full and we talk about packing it in before the tide turns.

"One more go at it," William says.

"We're full up, son," Martin says.

"One more go. I want to work the deep end." William jogs to my pole and begins marching it out.

"Hell," Martin says, and picks up the beach pole. The other men are too drunk or tired. J-Hook's boy goes for the middle pole and Martin waves him off. "Joseph," he says, and I pick it up.

William's bobbing in the deep end and the net's tight but he's drunk and waving the pole all over.

"Plant it and drag back!" I yell. The wind is picking up, moaning in from the sound. William keeps trudging out deeper. "Too far, damnit!" He goes on, dragging us all out with him. I look back to the beach and Martin is up to his thighs and shaking his head, waving with his off hand. Up ahead, I can't see William. The net goes slack as he drops the pole somewhere ahead in the dark. "Shit."

I start swimming, one hand running along the line of the net. The tide's pulling out so I make way with ease. I find the pole and William's nowhere in sight. Then, out in the sound, I hear him sputter. In the moonlight, I see him flail. Gone and gone. That's what he'd be. A tragedy to some. Carey gets the house. I get Carey.

Martin's voice comes in on the wind with half of my name, and William sputters again. I drop the net and swim to where I hear the struggle. William latches on and the mass of him pushes me under the surface. He's panicked, climbing and scratching and gasping. I punch him in the nose and he quiets. I punch him again and he goes slack.

I get him halfway back, shouting, and Martin helps me drag him to the beach. The men circle. William's still and bleeding from the nose. J-Hook pushes on his chest a few times. Drunk Billy pushes him aside and performs CPR until William comes around, coughing and pushing Billy's face away. The men hug and shout. J-Hook's boy vomits up a belly of rum. William starts to say something, but the tide's running quick so we drag him by the fire and load the boat in a rush, the men pulling on thick briny sweaters as they go.

The near-drowned man sleeps in the bow and, sullen and alone, I watch him from the center console where Martin rubs my back. "Damn fine, brother," he says after he eases the motor down from a roar. Above the roofs and trees on dry land, I see the fat-shrimp-moon is almost set. Martin kisses my head and says it again. "Damn fine."

At the dock, we let William sleep. The men say their piece. Everyone hoots and shakes their heads and helps carry the heavy coolers up the ramp. Martin and I walk William to my truck and drive him to Carey's. I watch him through my rearview, slumped over in my backseat and snoring. He'll live to be a hundred, I know, and we'll just keep at it the way we do. Me and Carey and William. We'll keep on till one of us is dead.

"He told me Carey's pregnant," Martin says.

I can't think of what to do but drive.

"He said he damn near broke her leg he was so excited to hear it."

"Yeah."

"Leave it be, Joe. There won't be nothing left of you." Martin says, and I think how he's always been the smarter of us. The seine was his baby, to be true. "You're a young man."

Ahead, Carey's big house rises from the marsh and the oaks, new trees just come up in the past thirty years. Babies for oaks. They were thin as my wrist when we were children and some other snowbirds owned the place. They paid me good money to cut around those oaks special. I spread mulch around them twice a year. The cab of the truck gets washed in the mottled light that makes it through the full canopies of the young oaks and Carey steps out the front door to wave us in and even this morning, I know beauty when I see it. I guess I earned that dollar. I guess I made good.

"Life is long," Martin says, and hums out some damn song I don't know.

THE ALIENS WILL COME TO GEORGIA FIRST

Joanna is an alien; she tells me in the backseat of the Lincoln. She whispers it in my ear and nips the lobe. I ask her what type she is, the chest-busting kind or the kind that probes? She slides a hand around the top of my pants while she thinks. She dips a pinky into my belly button like a butterfly tongue, making noises as she does. Preep—preep—preep. I'm the probing kind, she says. With her fingers, Joanna traces the bulges and hollows of my throat. With her lips, she trails my collarbone with care.

When the time comes, blinking on the dashboard, we crawl to the front of the car and sit waiting on the defroster. Through the silver smears of the glass, I see the dogs of Showman's Cliff in the Lincoln's headlights. They're pacing between the picnic tables set up near the drop, the ones that look out over the forested pine slope and the yellow spots of the town below. Another dog slips into view, and then another. Left-outs. Last year's Christmas puppies, brought home with red ribbons stuck to their head and living full-time at Showman's before the summer, after they'd shit the rug that last damning time or eaten that one special whatever-it-was. For my aunt it was her mother's doilies. All that ancient yellow lace, passed down to *her*, to *Helen*, not to her sisters Justine or Sarah. She had fought for that lace after her mother's passing, and to see it then: shredded and trailing out in strings from the Labrador's puckered anus. It was too much for Aunt Helen. Jimmy, I think she called that dog.

I can see Jimmy in the headlights of the Lincoln, two years since his becoming a left-out, and Jimmy looks mean. With the hair on his back standing up in a ridge, and one of his floppy lab ears ripped away, snarling at a mutt who is snarling back. The fur is matted with black smears, badges of distinction won rolling in some fetid armadillo, some rotted raccoon, something that would never have been allowed if he had stayed Helen's dog. At least he has that.

Joanna cranks the window down, just a few inches, and Jimmy comes padding over all genteel now. No bad dogs live on Showman's for long, and Jimmy knows just how to hang his jaw, though there are teeth missing, ripped away. He knows how to smile.

When Joanna has Jimmy's attention, I crack my window and whistle. The other five strays pad over to the driver's door and jockey for position. On Joanna's side, Jimmy is alone, and Joanna, my girl, drops half a cheeseburger for him. She grins, her breath fogging the window, as he takes it in a single bite. Before we discovered this maneuver, when, before, we'd thrown dollar burgers out like confetti for the dogs, we'd seen the fighting. We'd seen a terrier with too much brass have his throat ripped out. It was safer to play favorites or not play at all.

Why won't you take him? she asks. I put the car into gear. I would take him, she says. If it were me living alone. You need something out there with you.

I've lived in my mother's trailer since she left for Atlanta and a job. I don't blame her. She'd managed a diner in town, gotten caught skimming, and after that—in a place this small—there wasn't any work to be had. But I'd finished school, I'd found a job at the hardware store, and Joanna was here with her folks; there wasn't anything in Atlanta that I wanted, so I stayed. I'm not home enough for a dog, I say, looking at the road. The Showman dogs are running alongside the Lincoln, sprinting ahead and crossing through the fog, dashing through the solid bars the headlights make. I have my foot dancing back and forth from gas to brake to keep from running them down.

Tell me some alien things, I say, and Joanna tells me that the aliens will come to Georgia first. She says they will come, not in saucers, but on their own, shipless and drifting like snow. How will they survive entry? I ask. Joanna says they will slide through the vacuum and the exosphere like fish, that the aliens will make themselves very thin. And when they come, they will float through the clouds with their toes all long and reaching for the tops of trees and the roofs of houses. They'll latch on to whatever they can and start to grow down, their toes like roots burrowing into the earth, and they'll lift their hands so their fingers knit together and blot out the sun. Joanna reaches across the cab and rests her hand on the back of my neck where my hair grows to my shoulders and curls into waves. She says this hair is wasted on me. She would like to steal it.

Why will they come to Georgia? Joanna says it is our soil they will want. Clay like cream. Porous sand. The granite boulders, hidden in the earth like dinosaur eggs. The alien toes will curl around them in the earth. Like anchors. And they're like plants, I say. No, she says, they're like fish. And they talk like dogs. You'll want to have one with you when they come. To interpret.

There is a plan by the town to remove the Showman Cliff dogs. The pack has grown, and people (people like Joanna and me) have been feeding them. Not just burgers, but proper food too. I know a boy who rides a four-wheeler to the picnic tables with a sack of dog feed bungeed to the back rack. When he gets to the dogs, he makes a long cut in the bag and does donuts until it's empty. All the dogs run after him, nipping at the tires. After the boy leaves, the dogs graze in the big, loose circles of dirt and dog food. And there are other folks like that. Folks who care for or profit off the dogs. The dentist who administers rabies vaccines to any dog he can catch. A woman who comes to play for them with her guitar. Ned Rigby, who, aside from owning the hardware store, runs a small hot air balloon operation and carries tissue paper kibble bombs in his basket. For a dollar, you can throw them to the dogs.

The plan to remove the dogs comes from a local cabal, the Daughters of the Confederacy, who have a lodge near Showman's and claim to own the cliff. *Though we, the Daughters of the Confederacy*, they wrote in their notice, posted all around town, *have allowed for some time the use of our cliff-side view and picnic tables for the enjoyment of the public, we have demanded that the dangerous animals left there be arrested, disposed of, or otherwise removed within the month.* And then came the threat: *Should the animals remain, we will have them KILLED and the land will be closed to public use.* The way the Daughters typed out "KILLED" in all capitals reminded me of an old west poster. WANTED. DEAD OR ALIVE.

People were upset, but the land was, the sheriff confirmed, private. In the weeks following the notice, some people took a few of the dogs in, the ones with both ears who still came when you called "Hey Boy" or what-have-you. The ones left now are the last of their kind. KILLED, I think. I can see it floating in the fog above the road, like the burn-shadow left in your eye after seeing a bright light: KILLED.

We are almost out of the pines and on to the main road. The way down from the cliff is slow going. The land is rooty and steep. So you work a lot, Joanna says. Jimmy'll sit at home. If he chews up something, who cares. And if he shits on the floor, you'll pick it up. He'll be alive. You're going to love him, she says.

I can see Jimmy in the front of the pack in the rearview. In the taillights, his fur is red. It is a new moon, and it occurs to me that when the lights of the Lincoln are gone, the dark here will be near complete. Where do the dogs go? I wonder. Do they seek light to sleep near, even if it's far away? If not the moon, then the Texaco star? Do they truce their quibbles for the night and huddle for warmth in eye-shot of the glow?

Where will you be in all this, I ask Joanna. With me and Jimmy and all the shit on the floor?

I'll be with you.

***

When Jimmy and Joanna moved into my mother's mobile home, things changed for me. For the better. Things that had been broken, Joanna fixed them. The screen door that wouldn't close and banged in the wind all night; she put in a new latch. The bed that lilted to one side; she threw out the busted boxspring and propped the thing up on cinderblocks and boards. The musk of the place, all the smells of my mother, she removed the blackout curtains and burned it all away with the sun.

Her first week in the trailer, Joanna cut a long "moon window" into the ceiling, screwed a sheet of Plexiglass over the hole, and caulked it all around. When the aliens come, she said, I want to see them. We lay together on the couch, watching the slim moon rise and the sky grow dusty. How sweet it is to have the natural light, Joanna said. How sweet it will be in the morning. And I said, I love it, but I was looking at the tops of the pines through the Plexiglass and imagining them crashing through and already feeling noon bake us.

Jimmy followed Joanna in the narrow alley of the mobile home, always underfoot and scrambling on the linoleum to get out of the way. The first week, he destroyed our pillows and quilt. We patched the fabric with old work shirts, Joanna's and mine. When Joanna took contract work on Sundays, hanging a door or some such, Jimmy and I would commiserate over coffee and toast or else smoke under the mobile home's little awning and watch the road for her return. Week days, the three of us ate our eggs in a circle by the radio, and when Joanna and I got home from work at the hardware store, Jimmy would walk out to us, whole body wagging, from beneath the trailer, where he liked to spend the days in the shade. And it seemed clear that we were, all three of us, deep in love. But at night, things were different.

Joanna slept poorly. She wouldn't stand to be touched or even to be lain near for her thrashing. Once she clawed her collar bone, her leg, my back. I woke to us bleeding, her shouting. She'd said she was falling, that she had fallen from Showman's and into the pines. We worried. Joanna kept her nails clipped short and took to sleeping in oven mittens. We bought a white noise cassette, then one titled Caribbean Summer, then took to AM radio, Weather and News. This helped some.

When Joanna stilled in bed, I would listen to the Doppler and the clicking of Jimmy's claws. Sometimes he would let out a grumbling whine that Joanna called a "mutter." More than once, I found him standing on the counter with his head up to the moon window and his shoulders knotted, howling. This would wake Joanna and start our sleepless cycle over again. I'd come stomping out of the bedroom to talk him down. He would still for a while, lay down where he liked to lay. Feign sleep. After a few hours he'd start it up again, the howling—not at the moon but, seemingly, not at nothing. Like he was reaching out to old friends. Like he knew what was coming for them. Is it the aliens? I asked Joanna once. She said no.

I took to walking Jimmy at night after Joanna was asleep. Something to wear him out. Sleepwalking, Joanna called it. As in: Did you sleepwalk last night? And I'd say: Ayuh, and there's vanilla in the fridge. That's a ritual of mine and Jimmy's. We walk to the Gas n' Go and get a half pint of ice cream. I spoon out Jimmy's in the parking lot where he eats the whole glob of it at once, like a marshmallow. I eat a little myself, and pocket what's left for Joanna. She feels included that way. Before the ice cream, when Jimmy and I would walk the bobcat trails by flashlight and scare the joggers come hoofing out from town, she felt like she was missing out on the adventure. I tell her it's not all that, the walking and the midnight ice cream, though, secretly, they are my favorite times.

Will the aliens allow ice cream? I ask. When we live like mole-people under their dark regime. The aliens, Joanna says, will allow ice cream, and life may continue on in the dark. The aliens will use the sunlight to fuel their brains and the brains will flash signals to one another through the woven fingers and hands that cover the sky. And it will look like a firework show all day, every day. But who will grow the vanilla beans, I ask, and Joanna kisses me sweetly while we stand over the kitchen sink. It is late in the night, and I have just come home from walking Jimmy. I will make you an electric garden, she says, sleep-poor and faded. And we will grow our own.

***

It was near the end of the Daughters' month when my mother had come back from Atlanta for the weekend and had a few things to say. Things about the hole we'd cut in her ceiling and things about Joanna. You planning on marrying this girl? She asked me over cigarettes and coffee. Yes, I said. It was the first time I'd said it aloud. The alien girl, she said. From the lumber yard? That's just a thing we do, I said. Things we say. The alien stuff. You never had a thing?

I had a thing with your father, then I had you, she said. And he was a carpenter. Could build things. I'd thought you'd fool a nurse or a school teacher while you still had your looks. Move out of this can. Instead, you cut a hole in the roof. Shack with a loon. There's a girl at my Chilies. She just started. No ring. Blonde hair. Rich daddy.

Don't you think it's past time you worried about who I'm fooling? I asked. We've got money coming in. We've got the place looking better. It's the real deal.

My mother raised her eyebrows like I'd asked to have a friend over for the night. She extended her hand for the cigarette we shared—something we started when I was in high school and sneaking them from her purse. She'd caught me, told me to ask out loud for what I want. Why stay? she asked. Take the girl, but leave the town. I shrugged and she shrugged back. That's all you've got?

I know how things work here, I said. The way it was for you, it doesn't have to be that way for me. I reached for the cigarette and watched it flare in her mouth.

It's always that way, she said. This town never did anything for us, even before that shit with me at the diner. The folks that are moving in now, the way prices are going, you'll never buy a house. Your kids will go to school on the "stink bus." You'll see it smash them down. Remember that?

That was kid stuff, I said.

You'll get smashed down bringing someone their fucking dinner or washing their car or selling nails—whatever it is. You'll get smashed, and they'll build a swimming pool. And a big fence.

The rest of our cigarette hissed in my mother's coffee. She stirred with a spoon and watched the butt spin like a compass needle. She pushed the filter to the bottom of the cup.

I collected the mugs from the table. I don't care about that stuff, I said. You don't know you care, she said. I told her the rent was in the mail. She said maybe she didn't want it. Said maybe she'd sell.

***

To make matters worse, word had gone around town that the Daughters had engaged a few of their sons and husbands to shoot the remaining strays. Any that's left, we're to shoot, Ed Spars reported to me at the cash register of the hardware store. On the counter was a box of .22 longs. I don't like it, he said. I don't like it at all. But it's my Margaret's pa's pa's land, and she don't want no rabid dogs, no biters out there with the little ones running around. No sir.

It was the same run of talk I'd heard him ambush three other men with in the store, Ed had hit them with it—these weak lines—whenever he found them in the aisles, he'd come walking up, calling them by name and jangling the box of rounds. I doubt he even needed the bullets, as they are sold by the thousand. I think he came to apologize, or for someone to tell him no.

If you don't like it, why do it? I ask. Just run 'em off. Whip 'em if you have to. No, no, no, Ed Spars says. He is nearly sixty and resembles a confederate general garden gnome. My Margaret, she can't have them around. They'll come back and bite one of them little ones.

You haven't had any "little ones" out on that cliff in forty years, Ed Spars, Ned Rigby says from Paints. And those dogs ain't bit nobody. I had my own gran-boys up there last month. No, no, Ed Spars says. No sir.

It's $9.99 if you want the bullets, Mr. Spars, I say. But you might call animal control in Macon. See if they won't come out. No, no, Ed says. They won't come out. He pays and leaves, and Ned walks out behind him with the paint mix he was testing still open on the counter. Through the store's big windows I can see them having words in the parking lot, Ned throwing his hands in Ed's face, and Ed looking old but standing very straight, saying no, no, no, whatever-whatever.

I stand still, watching, wondering how far it will go. Ned knocks the box of cartridges from Ed's hands and they scatter like golden roaches on the concrete, then he waits for Ed to bend down to collect them, but he doesn't, he just stands fiddling with his beard and looking at the .22s where they glitter on the ground until Ned storms off to the lumber yard.

I go out to help Ed pick up his rounds. Not because I think it's right for him to shoot the dogs, but because he is an old and dignified man who would not fight in the hardware store parking lot, and because it wouldn't do to leave the mess.

When I call Macon Animal Control, the line is busy. I call back again, and it's the same. Ned comes back a while later and says he'd like to see Ed Spars in a ditch.

***

I don't know what happens when we die, but Joanna says most of us dissolve into the soil. That sounds about right to me. The day after Ed Spars comes for his .22s, we are eating burgers with Jimmy in the Lincoln at Showman's, discussing whether or not all dirt is dirt that once held a dead person. I'm fairly certain it has to be. I'm not sure, Joanna says. Is sand dirt? she asks. In my mind I see a pie chart projected on to the painted brick wall of a classroom. In it are the four components of soil: minerals, air, water, and dead people. I believe so, I say. Then we've been making dead-guy castles all this time, she says. And muddy dead-guy pies, I say.

The strays are off wherever they are, and Ned Rigby's big flat-bed truck is parked out by the cliff. On the back is the hot air balloon basket. The blowers are running and, before our eyes, an enormous red balloon inflates over the cliff, while Ned spits sunflower seeds out of the side of his mouth and fuels up the burner.

Jimmy huffs and lies down in the backseat. Then he gets up and hangs his head out of the window. Then he lies down again. He would like to get out of the car. I open the door for him, and he starts to patrol, sniffing the picnic tables, the legs of tree roots where they push out of the earth, the place where a bird has died. He pads over to Ned, who gives the dog's one good ear a rub. Five minutes now, Ned calls to us. In the car, Joanna has gone very still. I find her hands slick and cold. Hey now, I say. It's stupid, she says. To be afraid. I don't think so, I say. This will be her first time in the air. We have decided to help Ned find the dogs and drive them out of town. Joanna hopes the balloon will cure her dreams.

When the aliens come, I say, there won't be much room for the balloon, so I figure we had better make the most of things now. Last night we'd lain in bed talking about the ways we would be OK dying: Drowning, no. Laughing fit, no. Cougar attack, sure. Burning up entering Earth's atmosphere, we decided, had enough gravitas if we were allowed a final monologue transmission to the people of Earth with some light Aerosmith playing in the background, but regular burning, no. Hot air balloon explosion was deemed dramatic enough.

The idea is for Joanna to ride with Ned and search while I drive Joanna's pickup and wait for their call, the one that says "they're in the woods near the kaolin mine," or "they're tearing up trash near the railroad." In the truck is a sack of burgers. I'm planning on kicking in the door of the Macon pound.

Will you be alright? I ask Joanna, and she says she will.

The balloon fills, and Ned starts the flame. I tie Jimmy up to a pine so he won't tear the Lincoln's seats. Best not leave him out here, Ned says, and nods up the road where the Daughters' lodge and Ed Spars' home is. Should have left him at the house, he says. Joanna asks if Jimmy can come in the basket, and Ned opens a little whicker door for her and the dog to step inside.

I stand on the cliff's edge and watch them rise, first by inches, then by feet. I hear Ned telling Jimmy to lay down now, lay down. From forty yards below, Joanna looks like an alien. Not Joanna's tree aliens, but some of my own. Her face is a small bright spot above her woven whicker body and her hand is waving like the feathered mouth of a crab beneath a swollen red brain. She is tasting the air. They are moving in slow motion, rising until they enter one of the rivers of air that wash over us, invisible, every day. I marvel at Ned's balloon, and Ned for possessing it. A small piece of old wonder: man flies. I call Joanna's phone and she tells me it is beautiful and she is not so afraid.

From the cliff, the town of Issock glints through the pine forest. I admire the main road and the gravel tops of shops glowing gray, the few cars milling around and checkering the streets in their reds and blacks. I see where the yellow-green rectangle of the high school's field stretches, the red baseball diamond pushed into a corner of trees. I see the dense green spread where I know our home is, buried in the woods.

The night of my mother's visit, I cooked pork chops and macaroni. Joanna poured wine. Then something set us off, Joanna and me. We got to talking about the aliens and what sorts of houses we would have to build when they finally came. My mother chugged her wine and asked if we were both cracked and had we made up any savings and were we using condoms when we screwed? This dog is fine, but babies are different, my mother said. Babies are reality. Joanna had Jimmy up on her lap, all seventy-odd pounds of him. Do you know what you're doing? my mother asked. She reached to scratch Jimmy's back and shaggy yellow hair filled the air. Yes, Joanna said. We do.

We gave my mother the master. On the couch that night Joanna whispered that when the aliens come, Jimmy will speak, and he will tell us what to name our children. I was lying on the cool floor. Why does he get to decide? I asked her. What would you name them? she asked. Mel, I said. Or Francis. My girl, she laughed like a jackal, while Jimmy snored.

When we saw my mother off in the morning, she told me why she'd made the trip. The place is already sold, she said. You've got two weeks. With her head out of the window and the car in reverse, she told me. Come to Atlanta, she said. There's work.

It's not so much leaving the trailer that bothers me. With Joanna and I working, there are places we can go. With Joanna's folks or in some little place. It was the how and why that stung. It was my mother's weighing and measuring that hurt when I ladled the soup I'd been simmering and sat across from Joanna to pass the news.

***

I'm putting Joanna's truck down Main, looking down the side streets for flashes of fur. I drive the half-hid places where the strays sometimes go. The loading bay of the grocery store. The low apartments across from the high school, where the strays race alongside pet dogs with a fence between them, goading and snapping and laughing the way dogs do. The strays are not to be found. I imagine them piled somewhere by Ed Spars, or somewhere in the pines, lain in the strange pattern of their killing. Or, more likely, black bagged in a dumpster.

Joanna calls. They're in the Ruby Hills lots, she says. Hurry. I look out of the window and see Ned's red balloon set against a sheet of high-cloudless. The basket is a thumbnail. Joanna is a fuzz.

Ruby Hills is a new neighborhood going up on the edge of town. The contractors and crew there are the best customers we have. I see all the things Issock can wrap up and sell littering the spaces between the concrete foundations. Burger wrappers and drink cups. Cigarettes and cigarillos. Hundreds of plastic ties from around our lumber, the boards themselves made into trusses and studs or heaped in great blocks. Across the lot I hear barking. Five or so dogs are play fighting by the green hulk of a materials dumpster. I ease the truck through the site, calling out the window, lobbing a burger into the group of them and watching it disappear.

The strays form a mass and edge around me. They are not snarling. They are whimpering. Their heads are going from high to low. One, I see is still laying by the dumpster, and there is blood caked to the fur all about his belly. Another has a limp. I see the small wound in the leg. The poor shot Ed Spars took with his .22 longs, wherever he found the pack in the night. Come on now, I say. I tear the wrapper off another burger, pull it apart, try to toss a piece to each dog. They follow me to the back of the truck, and leap into the bed when I toss one, two, three burgers inside.

Yeah! I hear Joanna from far off, see them descending.

I close the tailgate and throw the burger bag at the dogs, while they eat, I pull the tarp we have fixed to Joanna's truck overtop the bed, fastening it to the wheel wells with bungie cords, smacking the heads and noses that protrude from beneath the heavy nylon folds. And the dogs resemble children caught in a pillow fort, their heads making hills and valleys in the tarp while I fasten it tighter, sides and back. They are barking and fighting and now howling, and I can hear Jimmy howling and barking too. Ned has the balloon low enough for me to see him and Joanna over the basket, and Jimmy too, his paws and his head, how it is upturned and long and desperate in its baying.

Yeah! Joanna yells again, and I am waving, and she and Ned are waving back, and Jimmy is calling to the dogs, who are calling out to anyone and no one, shrill and desperate, and then I see Jimmy leap from the basket, soaring, his legs kicking and his body in a twist and still barking mad as he slips through the sky, cleaving the air, reaching out for the red clay and the tops of the pines and the skeleton houses below.